JAN SLEPIAN

LESTER'S TURN

MACMILLAN PUBLISHING CO., INC.
New York
COLLIER MACMILLAN PUBLISHERS
London

Macmillan Publishing Co., Inc.
866 Third Avenue, New York, N.Y. 10022
Collier Macmillan Canada, Ltd.
Printed in the United States of America
10 9 8 7 6 5 4 3 2 1
LIBRARY OF CONGRESS CATALOGING IN PUBLICATION DATA
Slepian, Janice B
Lester's turn.
SUMMARY: When 16-year-old Lester, himself a
victim of cerebral palsy, takes his retarded friend
from the hospital for the weekend, tragedy ensues,
forcing Lester to examine the real meaning of their
relationship.
[1. Friendship—Fiction. 2. Cerebral palsy—
Fiction. 3. Physically handicapped—Fiction.
4. Mentally handicapped—Fiction] I. Title.
PZ7.S6318Le   [Fic]   80–29467   ISBN 0–02–782940–5

To Rosie

CHAPTER ONE

I didn't kill my friend Alfie, but sometimes in the dead of night, I still feel I gave him a shove. What I wanted to do, tried to do, was kidnap him.

I didn't have that idea in my head at all that morning. It was just my usual Saturday visit to the hospital and the last thing in the world I was thinking of. I knew I was troubled about him. What I mean is, I was desperate. But I didn't know I was also crazy.

I had called Claire to meet me at her station. When I have something on my mind, she's the one I talk to. What I wanted was for her to come with me to the hospital to see for herself what Alfie had become. Maybe she'd have some idea of what to do. She had moved from the old neighborhood a month or so before, and it was just an easy bus ride from her station to Alfie's.

That's how come she was waiting for me that morning at the bottom of the elevated steps. She waved, and I stood there looking down the long flight of steps for a moment, as I suppose skiers do before throwing themselves off some terrible hill. I saw a clear space ahead. Gangway! Watch out! Here I come! Once I push off, there's no stopping. That's how I go down steps and that's that. Whoever it is that watches over stubborn cripples sees to it that I don't fall . . . too often. I don't know why, really, since other times a crack in the sidewalk, a matchstick, a hiccup, anything can bring me down. One of my life's minor miracles. Sometimes it's the other people, scattering like buckshot to get out of my way, who do the falling. It's the look on their faces as they see this . . . this *thing* bearing down on them. What is it? A drunk? A loose crazy? I know how I must look: arms whipping the air, face twisted with the effort, rubbery legs, everything flapping away as I plunge down full tilt. The climbers, hearing the racket, look up and make a dash for the sides, like getting away from an avalanche. And as I pass them, I sense the alarm and disbelief, and pity, of course, and all the rest of the junk I've gotten used to in my sixteen years.

Claire was doubled up when I got to her. Can you believe it? "You've got some sense of humor, you know that?" I said when I caught my breath.

And there we were, not having seen one another in over a month, and already we were laughing together.

"Yeah, I know," she said. "It's my best feature." She took my hand and swung it back and forth. "Hey, Lester, I'm glad to see you. You're still a shrimp." That's a joke we had because we were both string beans and the same height: too tall. I seemed to get taller all the time, and all it meant to me was that there was more of me to wave around. "You still look like the Prince of Wales." That was an old dig at my blond hair and long nose. She always thought I looked "English," whatever that meant.

She looked the same to me. Still didn't wear lipstick or fuss with herself that I could see. Still the same old shorts and T-shirt under the jacket, still all bones and angles, big hands, big feet, straight brown hair always falling in her eyes to be scraped back by spread fingers.

She saw me looking at her and immediately crossed those clear gray eyes and made the face that used to send us all into fits.

She wasn't paying the least attention to the few people standing around watching us.

"They think you're a mean, rotten person laughing at one of God's poor creatures," I said, pushing my head their way.

She laughed again. "I know. But that's some show you put on. You should charge admission. Can't you hang on to the railing or something? I mean, wouldn't it be easier? Not that I would want to miss that scene for the world. I could use you on my team. Next week we play Erasmus High, and if only they could watch you come down steps when the score got close! We'd win hands down. They'd be hysterical."

"Very funny!" That's our way. She teases me and I pretend to be indignant. She's the only one who fools around with me like that. Most people make me feel like I come from the moon. Either they are overcareful, speaking to me as if I were deaf or three years old, or else they avoid me like I had a bad case of hoof and mouth disease instead of this perfectly ordinary, noncontagious cerebral palsy.

We stood there in the crowded street, and since this was the first time for me in that part of Brooklyn, there

3

was plenty to see. Small shops lined the wide avenue. Shoppers were out in droves with kerchiefs on their heads and shopping bags in their hands. The March wind blew the litter around and made my eyes water. It was busy, busy, full of grime and motion.

Claire pulled my arm while I was looking around. "C'mon home with me, Les, just for a while. We can talk there. Wait till you see it! A real house—can you imagine? Well, it's a two family, but not a big old apartment house with millions of people like the old place."

There was something about her tone.

"Hey, what do you mean? The old place isn't so bad. I still live there, remember?" I don't know what got into me. All of a sudden, I was shaky. It was the word "remember." It scared me that with Myron and Claire moved away and Alfie stuck in a hospital, I was the only one remembering old times. Better times.

I said, "Let's get to the hospital first. I'll see your house some other time. I want to talk to you about Alfie. I want you to see him. You haven't been there in ages."

She shook her head. "Can't go, Les. Sorry. I forgot that Blanchie was coming over this morning and we're going to my friend Jean's. Jean Persico? I haven't told you about her yet. Besides, I thought Alfie was okay in that place. What are they doing, beating him?"

"No, they're not beating him, Claire." So new friends were more important than old ones! "If you're not coming, I've got to go." My lips felt too stiff to talk and I was too jangly to stand there much longer.

Claire saw how it was with me. "Look, what are you doing tomorrow? Come on over and I promise we'll talk

4

nonstop about Alfie. Except for one little bit. I've got something terrific to tell you! You gotta see what's upstairs from me!" She hugged my arm and grinned at me and whatever was hurting in me stopped. She placed my hand on top of her head. "I have to go to work now. I'm a Music Hall Rockette and they are waiting for me onstage." She kicked her leg higher than my hand, easy for her with those stilts of hers sticking out of her shorts like stork legs. She was in some good humor, and when Claire feels good, there is no one like her. The newspaper man in his little booth next to the grocery called out, "Very good, young lady. Some kicker you are." Claire said to him, "Miss America of 1939," and curtsied and blew kisses to the air and we all laughed.

That act was all for me. When she wanted to she could always make me feel better.

A bus swung by, and stopped. Number 17. It was mine and I hauled myself on it.

The hospital is a whole collection of big brick buildings. One of the buildings was a regular hospital and the others were just caretaking places for people who can't get well from whatever it is they have. Like Alfie. You can get very lost if you don't know which building to go to. I always felt I could wind up in a bed if I wasn't careful. On the outside I don't look too different from some of the patients.

And what's my friend Alfie doing in a place like that! Okay, he's slow in the head and slow because of the limp. And okay, he gets epileptic fits once in a while. That sounds like a barrel of laughs to have for a friend, right?

5

Like being pals with a case of gangrene? But believe me, if you saw him or knew him, it wasn't like that at all. We had plenty of laughs, plenty of good times together. Things happen. You turn a corner and nothing's the same. I still can't get over it. When his mother died, I thought my eyes would fall out of my head I felt so bad. After that, his father, Mr. Burt, put him here because of the traveling job. The kid brother is with some aunt, and *whooosh,* the family I knew is gone. And now Alfie sits here like a bundle in the Lost and Found.

I went through the gate, nodded to the guard in the booth at the entrance and walked the path to the first building on the square. It looked something like my high school, but once inside, the smell didn't come from coeds. I can't figure out what it is, as many times as I've been there, and it's always the same. As close as I can come, it's a combination of chicken soup and urine. How's that for appetizing? Lunch anyone?

Near the elevator, I nodded to the guy in the wheel-chair who has sat in the same place ever since I started going there. More than a year now. He gets the people coming in the door and sells raffle tickets and newspapers. He's like me. I mean, he has cerebral palsy. Except he can't walk and I'm sure he's feeble-minded. That's why he's there, of course. Must be in a bad way. Not like me at all, really. I didn't like the sight of him.

"Buy a raffle?" he asked me every time.

"No, thanks."

"Buy a newspaper?"

"No, thanks." I waited for the elevator to creep down, pulling on it in my mind. One of the inmates, I mean patients, ran the thing, and even I could walk up the four flights faster than that thing ran.

I got to Alfie's ward and he was gone. I left my jacket on the bed and started looking, going first to the lounge where the radio was. Not only was he not there, no one else was either. Usually, it's full of wheelchairs and men in bathrobes, talking or not talking to one another, sitting at tables, playing cards, dozing. Sick, aimless men. It's full of sights I don't want to see.

I stopped a nurse on the run. "Where's Alfred Burt?"

"Everyone is down in the chapel."

CHAPTER TWO

I pushed open the door to the chapel. What I saw was a lot of color and what I heard was a lot of noise. I had walked in to a party! It was like some queer New Year's Eve! The color came from the sun shining through the stained glass windows and from the fancy hats everyone was wearing. The noise was for the guy up on a platform with an accordion slung around his neck. He was bowing, and everyone who was able was clapping away or blowing one of those paper horns that roll out like a long tongue. There was a big cleared space in the middle of the room where some volunteers were walking around helping to whoop it up.

I spotted Alfie on a chair across the room, but there was no way to reach him except by crossing the cleared space. I felt like a fool. One of the volunteers stopped me and said, "Too bad you're late. I'll find a seat for you." See? Right away they think I'm a patient. I told her I was there to see a friend, and I made my way to Alfie. He was busy, busy eating away from a paper plate on his lap. He didn't see me.

How could someone so energetic, so wiry and hopping, change so? I could see his belly pushing against the gaps of his shirt, and the top of his pants couldn't close. Fat and soft and shoveling in ice cream. Alfie, who used to be so busy all the time noticing things, picking them up, putting them down, laughing, always wanting to work, my *friend*, for Chrissake! Now he just sits and shovels in food like some greedy baby.

I touched his shoulder. "Alfie," I said.

He looked up, his eyes empty, uninterested. For an instant, he didn't recognize me. Then he smiled and said with his mouth full, "Oh-oh, Lester, looka here." He showed me his plate of party stuff like it was the prize of all times. He wasn't in the least surprised to see me, but then, he never was. I always felt I dropped out of his mind when I wasn't there, and when I next appeared, it was as if I'd never left.

A volunteer brought over a chair and I sat.

Alfie's face was the color of my ma's cookie dough. With that olive skin and head of black curls, he used to look like a healthy field worker, like he should be out picking grapes or something. I knew he didn't get outdoors much anymore. It wasn't his bad hand or leg so much as the epilepsy. A floor attendant once told me that even with drugs he still had fits. So the hospital didn't want to take the chance of his falling on the cement paths. It made things easier for them if he stayed inside. But Alfie lived for the outdoors. He never even noticed the weather. If only I could get him out of there somehow, we could walk and walk and walk, and he would get like he was before.

Alfie was intent on the stuff on his plate, so we didn't

talk. Besides, the entertainment wasn't over. The M.C. announced something. The piano struck up, and a little girl with curls like Shirley Temple came out and did a tap dance while singing "On the Good Ship Lollipop." She was so cute I wanted to vomit. Ooohs and aaaahs from the audience. Nothing like a little child to make the brains run out of the ears. Me, I would have stuffed the kid in a pillowcase.

The song finished, thank God, and the girl blew kisses and flashed her dimples a lot. The volunteers and nurses then walked around the cleared space clapping and trying to get everyone else all fired up, too. It was like they were cheerleaders at a football game.

"Hey there, Mrs. Levy. Let's hear a little applause. Isn't she adorable?"

"Wake up, Sidney, this is no time for sleep. It's a party. Did you hear that little girl sing? An angel or not?"

The child ran off the platform, and then came a lady wearing a long dress and a hat and gloves. She stood by the piano, and for one joyful moment, I thought she might lift it up as part of a juggling act. Instead, she sang. She had the kind of voice with a shake in it on every note; I could picture a little man in there rattling her vocal cords like they were bars in a jail. If I were there with Claire, we'd get the giggles. I just looked around and tried not to hear.

"What a scenery!" as my aunt, better known as Dumb Dora, would say. That was an audience out of some sick dream. Half of them weren't paying attention, heads sunk on their chests, those awful paper party hats, like little kids wear, slipping down over an ear or nose. They seemed weighed down by sleep or boredom, or both. Maybe a party doesn't help all that much. Of course, there were others, men and women sitting on chairs, some in regular clothes, eating and talking, enjoying the show, having a good time like at any party. But all my eyes could see were the sad ones.

Someone handed me a plate of ice cream and cake, and when I looked up to see who it was, I cheered up immediately. She was so comical looking. She was a young girl, maybe not more than thirteen or fourteen, and one of the volunteers because she was wearing a pink smock. She was the roundest little thing I ever saw, cheeks and arms and all the rest so chubby you wouldn't think she had a bone in her body. Her hair was a fright, that frizzy kind that looks like it was struck by lightning. It was gathered by rubber bands into two clumps on either side of her head. She wore thick, black-rimmed glasses, so I could barely make out her eyes. She was so full of smiles and good humor they almost disappeared behind those big red cheeks.

"Can I get you anything more? Something to drink maybe?" High and breathless, her tone said, "Oh, please let me be of service, oh, please like me."

"You want a drink, Alfie?" I asked.

"Yeah." I guess with nothing much else to do, food gets important.

I told the girl two Cokes, and she dashed off as if given the mission of her life.

Next was a magic act and I gave it all my attention, because they are my favorites. I love to watch the hands moving, moving, smooth as fish through water. Such perfect control is magic enough for me. The magician was a young guy, pale and sweaty under his ratty, black top hat. Must have been his first time there. I could see the big half-moons on his shirt when the cape fell back. Poor guy, he wanted everyone to join in, everyone to be part of the act. He didn't have the audience for that.

He asked someone in the first row for a quarter. The coin danced for a beautiful moment on his knuckles and then *pooof!*, it disappeared. Where was it? we all were asked. Somewhere in back of me an old voice shouted, spiteful and pleased the voice was, "On the back of the left hand. Look there. That's where the *momzer* keeps it!"

Poor magician, so it was. Then, a rope cut in two by a lady patient, who needed help with the scissors, was miraculously joined once again. The rope, completely healed, ah, so easy, was dangled well and whole in front of us. Gasps and applause for the lucky rope. Once again, the sour voice in the back said, "Old as the hills that one. The *schlemiel* cut a loop, that's all. No rope, just a loop. Older than me, that trick!"

I had to laugh with the rest, but really, the whole thing just depressed me more.

After that, the entertainment seemed to be over, because the M.C. was thanking everyone for being such a great audience. He said his lodge was proud to bring such beautiful entertainers there, and let's hear it for them. The cheerleaders came onto the floor for a final rousing.

"Come on, everyone! Let's hear that applause!"

I saw my girl working her way around them holding

two bottles with straws sticking out of them. She handed them over and was still beside us when the party broke up.

We handed her back the bottles, and she beamed those red cheeks at me and said, "I know you. I see you around the neighborhood, lots. I live in Brighton Beach, too."

"You do?" I turned to Alfie and was about to say, "Hear that? She lives near us." He was sitting . . . looking at nothing, emptied, stopped like a clock. Maybe it was that sight, maybe it was almost saying "near us" and realizing there was no "us" any more, maybe it was saying to myself before, "If only I could get him out of there somehow." It may have even been the girl standing there so eager to please. Whatever it was, I was seized by an urge that half lifted me from the chair. I would just walk Alfie out of there right then! Just walk him out! Just take him home with me. A kidnapping was about to take place! And this willing girl standing next to me, smiling at me like she would do anything at all, she would be my accomplice.

I told the girl I wanted to talk to my friend for just a few minutes. Would she please, please, come back in just a little while. I wanted to ask her something very important. I thought maybe she could hear my heart thump.

Her eyes widened so I could see the little black dots. She absolutely would, yes, of course, she was . . . be right back and yes, talk to my friend and she would be right there, oh, yes.

Anyone that smiley and friendly and willing would

surely help me get Alfie out of there. If only those cold fingers would get out of my chest.

When she turned away, I pulled my chair closer to Alfie and said, "How would you like to come home with me?"

He looked at me blankly. "Home?" he said, just as if the word didn't mean anything to him. Then the look in his eyes changed, and he said "home" again, only this time it meant something.

"We'll go to my house," I said urgently. "You'll stay with me. It'll be all right with my ma. We'll walk around the way we used to, remember? We'll go to the beach, and we'll collect stuff again. We'll be together. How about it, Alfie?" I had no idea if my ma would let him stay. I had no idea beyond getting him out. It was like talking in a dream.

"Sure, Les." This time there was his old open-mouthed grin. He trusts me, needs me. Anyone could see that.

"All right then, let's go."

CHAPTER THREE

I waved to my girl, who was over by the door watching us. Most everyone had cleared out of the chapel, and only the workers were left, picking up the paper plates and discarded hats.

"What's your name?" I asked her when we walked over to her.

"Tillie-Rose," she said. "I know yours. It's Lester, right?"

I nodded.

"I know him, too. I know Alfred. I've seen him around. I've seen you both, because I help out here on weekends. Can I tell you something?"

"Sure."

"I just want you to know I think you're wonderful. I think what you do is noble!"

"Yeah? Ah, sure. Sure thing. What is?"

"You coming all this way to see your friend. Two of you, two friends separated by fate, and you, loyal to the end." She clasped her hands in front of her as if I were an altar. "I just wanted you to know how I feel, that's all." She blinked at me through those thick glasses.

"Well, ah, thanks there, Tillie-Rose." For a second, I forgot what I was going to ask her. I didn't want to interrupt the flow, so to speak. All those good things coming out of her mouth. I ate it up. At the same time, I wanted to laugh at her. "Since you feel that way, would you do me a little favor?"

"Oh, anything! Anything."

Then I told her what I had in mind. All I wanted was to take Alfie home with me. Out of the hospital and home with me. If she would just come with us to the gate to tell the guard it was perfectly okay, I would appreciate it. She didn't have to do one thing more. Just that little bit, and that's it. That wasn't asking much, especially since she thought I was such a hero.

Well, you'd think I was asking to take *her* home with me. Poor girl, those little blackberry eyes opened up and she looked scared to death. She clasped her hands together again, this time as if begging for help. "Oh, gee! Oh, gee, you can't do that! I mean, I can't do that! I'd love to help you and all, but you, you, I mean, only parents maybe, only with permission from the office. You just can't do that! What about his medicine and all? You mean just take him . . . without . . . ?"

She was floundering. She didn't know how to deal with this nut case she suddenly had on her hands.

"Okay, okay, calm down. Can't you take a joke? I was only kidding."

Whew, what I got myself into for just asking a little favor. I felt so absolutely sure of what I wanted to do that nothing she said made a dent. If she wouldn't help, I'd do it alone. If I were eight feet tall with muscles like basketballs, I couldn't be more sure. I don't know what came over me, but nothing, not medicines, not guards, not what about after, was going to stop me. It was as if just my wanting it so bad was going to take care of everything.

"Tell you what," I said. "If you really want to help, you can get my jacket off Alfie's bed on the fourth floor. You know where his bed is? You'd be doing me a great favor, Tillie-Rose. We'll wait right here. Take your time."

You never saw anyone look so relieved. She was so glad to get off so easily. "Sure thing," she said. She looked like she was about to thank me for letting her help with something, at least. Instead, she said, "Back in a sec."

I hoped not.

The chapel was on the ground floor. Down the hall was the main entrance to the building. All we had to do was to get there.

The hallway was filled with people. The party was over, but patients were still hanging around, talking things over or heading for their floors. Since it was a weekend, there were also a lot of visitors standing around, coats and hats over their arms, talking in that cheery way people have when visiting the sick. They looked about as different from the parent or relative they were visiting as the man in the moon from the rest of us. It didn't matter whether the visitors were old or young, they were another story from the inmates. Something else, poles apart. How could I ever be taken for a patient when I knew, palsied as I am, there was an ocean between me and anyone inside that place?

Anyway, it was all to the good that it was crowded. We would be noticed less.

"Excuse me, excuse. Let us through, please."

I did a lot of excusing, hanging on to Alfie's hand, working my way through the crowd. Finally, we were through the mess around the door of the chapel, but I could see ahead another large group waiting for the elevator. Just beyond the elevators and around a corner was the exit.

Alfie tugged his hand away just as we were almost past the elevator crowd. Someone had called his name. For one awful moment I thought it was Tillie-Rose. For all I knew, she could fly up to the fourth floor and back down again in no time. It wasn't Tillie-Rose. It was a lady patient in a wheelchair.

"Alfie, Alfie, take me up," said the patient. Not even a please. She was a tiny thing, except for her large head, which looked as if it could have sat on a wrestler. Her legs were covered by a blanket, or maybe she didn't have any. But what I could see of her, her arms especially, were like a four year old's. The saddest thing about her was a perky pink bow in her hair. That could have made me cry, except I was furious with her. At a time like this, when I was in an absolute sweat to get out of there, she wanted Alfie to push her into the elevator and take her upstairs someplace. And what did Alfie say to this?

"Yeah, sure. What floor do you want?"

"Alfie, no! We have to go!"

He didn't understand. There was no use explaining.

18

He would never do anything against the rules or do anything wrong—knowingly, that is. If a grown-up told him to do something, he did it. That's how he was. He didn't pay any attention to me. He would get his mind set on something, and then nothing could budge him. I knew that.

I couldn't believe what was happening. All the courage I started with was leaking away as the elevator moved upward. I could picture Tillie-Rose waiting for us when we got back down again.

We deposited Pink Bow at her floor, but when we were able to return to the ground floor again, Tillie-Rose was not to be seen.

So, once again, I took Alfie's hand and headed for the exit. By the time we reached the lobby, I was beginning to breathe easier.

There was always a bunch of people sitting near the door in the lobby, just watching who came in and who went out. It was their show, their entertainment. Most of them were in wheelchairs. I could understand that that was maybe the most interesting thing they had to do in a place like that. So there was this greeting committee just when I would have liked to be invisible.

"Goin' out for a walk, hey, Alfie?"

"How ya doin', Alfie?"

"Where ya goin', kid?"

This time, Alfie laughed his good-natured laugh and didn't stop to talk. No one asked him to do anything, that's why. We'd be turning around and going up an elevator again if they had, I was sure. He kept holding on to my hand, not giving a second thought to leaving the place. It's a wonder he didn't stop and explain that I was taking him home.

I pushed open the door and we were outside. It was chilly without jackets, but not too bad. I knew Alfie never seemed to notice the cold, and I was too excited to think about such a little thing.

The grounds of the hospital were really nice—like a park, only more carefully tended. There were paths for walking and a lot of grass and trees and benches. On warm days, there were always plenty of people walking or being pushed along. But that day, for some reason, maybe because of the party, there wasn't anyone between us and the main gate, where we had to get by the guard.

Except Tillie-Rose. There she was, talking to the guard, looking up at him sitting in that booth. She had my jacket over her arm! With her was a white-coated orderly from Alfie's floor, a big guy named Harry, who I knew gave Alfie his bath.

I stood frozen still on the steps watching them. "The jig is up," I said to myself like Edward G. Robinson in the movies. I saw Tillie-Rose go out to the street and look up and down the block and then return to say something to the guard. Then, she and Harry went back inside the building through the nearest side entrance and that was that. They didn't come our way or see us. She didn't even leave my jacket with the guard. Some nerve!

So now all we had to do was get past the guard. I had an excuse all ready, made up on the spot. If he asked to see my pass for taking Alfie out, I would say I lost it and I would look so sincere that he would believe me. You see, I had this light-headed feeling that I could make things go my way no matter what. I had this feeling that if I just plowed ahead and did what I wanted to do, it would turn out all right because I wanted it so much.

It looked like that was going to be the case. A visitor came through the gate and started talking to the guard. The stranger evidently didn't understand some direction because the guard came out of his little booth to point to another building.

We were out the gate and on the street. We headed for the corner bus stop. I looked over at Alfie and felt so . . . elated. Like Superman. I had a twin bed in my room from the time Ma was so hopeful I'd be bringing hordes of friends home to stay over just like other kids. Never happened. But it was about to. I was bringing someone home for the twin bed. Alfie was not exactly what Ma had in mind, since even when he lived home, Ma never liked to see us together. Half the time I didn't even tell her I had been to visit him. But I was going to make it all right with her. "You'll see," I told her inside my head. "It will all work out. You'll see," I told myself. I was the nervous magician telling off that know-it-all, spoil-it-all voice in the back row.

We were almost to the corner, almost to the bus, when I heard Alfie's name called and the pounding of feet behind us. When I turned around, I saw the guard, two orderlies and my good pal Tillie-Rose running after us.

CHAPTER FOUR

Considering that the penalty for kidnapping is death, I got off easy.

I was hustled to the director of the hospital, Mrs. Brenner, a small woman in a big office. What I did was to play dumb.

"Whatever did you have in mind?" she asked me mildly. We sat across from one another with the desk between us. I picked on a button of my jacket, which Tillie-Rose had returned to me, and gave her my baby-blue stare. "Oh, nothing much. I was just going to take Alfie home with me for a little while and return him later." Like a deposit bottle. "Isn't that okay?" I asked. Real dumb act.

She looked at me hard, trying to size me up. After all, I looked like a candidate for her hospital. How tough could she be with me?

She was just a plain, motherly looking woman, like she could be one of the ladies in Alfie's building, sitting by an old husband's bedside knitting away at something end-less and ugly. Except this one had something about her that would make you jump when she said jump. I felt she knew what color my underwear was and what I had for breakfast.

She kept looking at me, fiddling with the glasses that hung from a string around her neck. Then she pushed her chair away from the desk. The chair had rollers on it so she could swing it around to look out of the window.

"Come over here, Lester," she said. Not a voice to fool around with.

The Venetian blinds were up, and we looked out of the window together for a few ticks of the clock. "Nice place you got here," I said.

She ignored that. No sense of humor, I thought, beginning to feel a little smug, getting away with my dumb act and all.

"This is a big place," she said. As I said before, not many people were out on the grounds, but there were a lot of buildings to look at.

"Sure is," I said, agreeing fast. Maybe we could just have a talk about maintenance, how much the light bill was, troubles with the help, important stuff like that.

"What do you think would happen if just anyone could walk in here and take out one of the patients without our knowing it?"

"I don't know." I really didn't. Search me. What's more, I didn't give a damn about those other patients. Let them out, let them in, it was only Alfie I wanted to save. Yes, save! I had to bite my lips from spilling it all out. About how Alfie was being wasted here. A good person like that! He was just fed and taken care of and given silly busywork to do like a pet hamster I once had. That little animal raced around at first, too, just like

Alfie did when he first came here. Then the hamster settled down at the bottom of the cage, just eating and sleeping, all the pep gone. I was trying hard not to feel, not to groan aloud at having been caught just when we were so close. Close to being together again. Feeling was for later. Now was only stupid time.

"Don't you know you must get permission to take out a patient? Permission from this office, permission from the family of the patient, all kinds of arrangements must be made about medicines, et cetera? Wouldn't that strike you as likely?"

I blinked at her. "Oh. I didn't know. Gee, I'm sorry. Next time I'll ask. Boy, next time I'll ask first."

Again, those eyes bored into me. Then, quietly, she said, "Now, Lester, you're smarter than that. I don't know what kind of game you're playing, but quit it and let's talk. Now tell me again. What did you have in mind?"

And that did it. What I had pent up a few minutes ago all spilled out. I don't know what kind of magic she had, but she got everything. By the time I was finished and was blowing my nose, she knew all that was on my mind and maybe more.

She sighed heavily. Then those sizing-up eyes looked at me with such sweetness, I thought I would melt to the floor like a candle. Don't tell me that you can't love a perfect stranger, an old lady at that. Maybe, given the right moment, you can love anybody.

Anyway, then it was her turn. She asked me how old I was and then told me when she was sixteen she tried to enlist in the navy as a sailor. "That had as much sense

to it as your trying to smuggle Alfie out of here today."
We shared a smile over that. She told me patients were
released to good homes all the time. Was that what I
had in mind? To take Alfie home and have him live with
me? Take care of him? I leaped at that. That's exactly
what I had in mind. I hadn't put it into words yet, but
that was it. I couldn't have said it better myself. In a single instant, I saw what I was doing when I kidnapped
Alfie. In a flash, I could see our whole future. I was going
to quit school and get a job and the two of us would live
together. I would take care of him. I would manage it.
My whole future—solved in one stroke, and all for Alfie's
sake! A great weight seemed to roll off me, a weight I
didn't know I was carrying.

And Mrs. Brenner had practically given me the idea.
Shown me the idea. She was on my side!

Well, not exactly. We were sitting across from one
another, the desk between us. Such a quiet lady, hands
clasped on her desk like a good child in school. "Never
mind *how* this would be done. What I want to talk
about is you. I don't think you know what is involved
here." And then she said things like: "He will always
need to be looked after." "He'll be tied to your future."
"He will hold you back." "Your mind is free in a way
that his is not."

Finally, she told me I had the right feeling but the
wrong idea. And when she said that, I saw clearly that
she may have the right idea, but she was the one with
the wrong feeling. At least she left out the feeling.

Talking with her only helped me see what I had to do.
She finished and we both stood up. I was surprised at

how little she was. She seemed so large and capable in that chair.

At the door, she said, "Take him out for a weekend, why don't you? Let him stay with you for a day or two. That would be splendid for him and good for you, too, my dear. Give you a taste of what it would be like. Do that. It could be arranged. Forget about taking him out for good!"

She looked up at me then and must have read my mind because she nodded her head and said, "I haven't convinced you of a thing, have I?"

It wasn't a question. She covered one of my hands with both of hers.

"Never mind, never mind. I know an obsession when I see one. Well, then I must tell you another thing— something practical. The state won't pay unless he's in a hospital. It doesn't pay for home care. It will take money to care for Alfie."

I hardly heard her. What I was thinking of was that in all her talk there was not one single mention of . . . what I was.

The last thing she said to me was, "Promise to come see me again."

Some lady.

I headed for the gate, longing for my room, on fire to plan my new life. I needed to talk to Claire, glad I would be seeing her tomorrow. I got to the gate and then turned back, wanting to see Alfie again. I just couldn't leave him like that. Maybe he was feeling awful. We hardly even said good-by when the orderlies took him away.

He was sitting on his bed playing solitaire.

"Hi, Alfie." I had to say it twice.

"Oh. Hiya, Les." He didn't have a thing in his voice, as if what happened just a short while ago never happened at all. He went on playing solitaire. We used to play war and maysha-paysha together. His face showed nothing. There was no life to him.

There suddenly flashed in my mind that scene in the drugstore, way back when. We were going around the neighborhood once, looking for pieces of wood for Myron, who was building a boat, when Alfie found a dollar. A whole dollar. He was always watching out for what he could find, because he was a great collector of things. Anything was a treasure to him—odd bits of string, cigarette wrappers, matchcovers, anything. Along the apartment houses on the street was a narrow strip of grass and bushes, all fenced in. Caught in one of the bushes was a dollar bill, and Alfie spotted it. Well, you should have seen his face! He used to throw himself entirely into whatever he was feeling so that when he laughed, he was all laugh from top to toe. "Hey, Les, looka here! Look what I found!" He waved it at me and threw back his head and was so gleeful you couldn't help but join him.

"What are you going to do with it, Al?"

This sobered him. He had to think, but not for long.

"I'll give it to my mother." She was the sun and the moon and the stars to him, poor lady. When I think how she would feel if she saw him now . . . . Well, anyway, I thought of something nice to do with the money.

"Why don't you buy her something with it?" I said.

This hadn't occurred to him. I knew that never in his

life—or in mine for that matter—did we ever have money to spend that way. "C'mon, let's go to the corner to Apatow's and you pick out something."

He was pulling the wagon that we used for the wood, and he wheeled it right into the drugstore, blocking the entrance. The guy behind the soda fountain told him to get it out of there in a hurry. I remember Mr. Apatow came out from the back, where he makes his prescriptions, and pulled the cart to the side of the door himself. Mr. Apatow looked like a gangster in the movies. It was those eyebrows like black, furry horns and his square face always needing a shave that made him look so fierce. He wasn't at all.

Mr. Apatow said, "What can I do for you today, Alfred?"

Everyone knew him. Alfie told him he was going to buy a present for his mother. He couldn't keep his voice down he was so excited. Mr. Apatow smiled, showing those big slabs of gray teeth and said, "What did you do, rob a bank?"

And then for the second time that day, Alfie was in heaven. You'd think never in his life had he heard anything funnier. By this time, everyone in the store was standing and listening and smiling. Such a simple thing to give such joy, just the way little kids are, the way we all were once. No wonder the rest of us had those silly smiles on our faces. It was like remembering way back when.

"You hear that, Les?" he said when he caught his breath. "That's a good one. 'Rob a bank,' he said. Boy, oh boy, oh boy." Lots of headshaking at how funny some people could be. Then again, "You hear that, Les? Wasn't that a good one?" Because he always had to make sure I was right there with him, in on whatever it was, right with him.

I don't remember what Alfie finally picked out—I think some face powder. And all the way home he was chuckling or shaking his head, or punching my arm, looking at the package, showing me the package, dizzy with delight, dragging his leg so fast I could hardly keep up with him. Full of life he was.

I felt so . . . sorrowful, looking at the lump he had become, sitting on his cot playing solitaire.

"Alfie, I'm sorry about today. Some other time we'll go home together. I promise. Okay?"

"Sure, Les. Some other time." He didn't even look up. He didn't care one way or the other. I could go or stay, it was the same. I went.

CHAPTER FIVE

Sunday morning was what I called hot rolls and scatter time at our house. Pa was up and out with the birds, preferring breakfast with them than with us. Most of the time, I didn't see him at all on Sundays since by the time I got myself out of bed, he was long gone. Sometimes in those early hours he must return and go out again because there is always that white bag of hot crispy fresh-baked rolls for Ma and me left on the kitchen table like a calling card, a hand wave that says, "I'm still here." Once I thought Pa and I were really going to get together. It no longer mattered. If he ever left for good and all, I think the only way I would know is that the white bag with hot rolls would stop.

Ma had her canasta group on Sundays, as sacred as church bells. They met at one house after another, like a chain letter, so most of the time I had the place to myself. I can't take notes in class, so usually I have tons of reading and memorizing to do.

That morning there was no schoolwork for me. I was dressed and ready to go to Claire's by the time Ma had come scratching and yawning out of her room. When Ma saw me she said, "Already? It's early yet. Where are you going? Fix your collar, Lester. Here, I'll do it. No homework today? When are you coming home?"

Most of Ma's questions I didn't have to answer. She asked so many at a time she forgot what came out of her mouth. She tugged at whatever was wrong with the jacket. She smoothed and patted and I thought I would scream with impatience. I don't know what was the matter with me. She used to be everything to me, and I would be scared stiff when she had to leave me even for a minute. But then . . . I don't know. I felt her waiting and watching all the time, and I only wanted to get away from her. I told her nothing.

I thought I'd never find Claire's house. When I turned off the busy highway on to her side street, the quiet surprised me. I felt like I was in the middle of a little kid's drawing. The small reddish brick houses on either side of the street, the trees lining the sidewalks were all the same, every one alike. I had the address in my hand and finally found her house in the middle of the block, a house no different from the rest, only the number changed. I couldn't imagine what it would be like to live in a place with just one other family. I couldn't imagine not hearing other people's noises, smelling what they were having for dinner, hearing their fights. No wonder Claire wanted to show off her house.

I rang the bell and no one answered. Twice more I did that and even banged on the door. I couldn't believe it—coming all that way and Claire not home! I turned to sit on the stoop for a while to think what to do, when I heard my name being called. I wanted to rub my eyes to make sure I was seeing straight, the way they do in the comics. Claire was coming down the middle of the street riding on a big black horse! She waved and, *clop, clop, clop,* there she was, looking down at me, holding the reins while the beast shook his head up and down like he was agreeing to eat me.

Claire put her nose in the air and said in her snootiest manner, "We just returned from the fox hunt, and tally-ho, old thing. Say hello to Mary."

I got brave enough to smooth the long black neck. "Claire, what in the world . . . ?"

She laughed and slid down next to me. Mary stood in the gutter like a parked car. "There's a stable around the corner on Avenue S where they keep horses for the vegetable men. You know the carts that come around with horses pulling them? Well, those horses are rented from the stable. They rest on weekends like the rest of us, right, Mary?" Mary got her nose kissed.

"So?"

"Well, so I shovel manure, and Gus, the man who owns the stables, lets me ride once in a while. He'll only let me ride Mary now because she's so easy, but soon he's going to let me ride Satan. Hey! How would you like a ride?"

"Are you kidding!"

"No, c'mon, I mean it. Get on. We'll ride you back to the stable. I'll walk you, don't be afraid. Mary couldn't go fast even if she wanted to."

"I couldn't!"

"Sure you could. You always *say* that. I'll take her up to

the house. You stand on the stoop there and I'll help you get up. You can do it."

Mary walked as slowly as a mourner back to the stable while I kept a death grip on the pommel. Never in my life did I ever expect to be on top of a horse. That Claire! I felt a thousand miles up. Stronger than the fear was the thrill. I felt such power under me. The force of it, the strength of it, was so beautiful. All that living, breathing power was me, was mine, from Claire's house to Mary's stable.

After that, everything else seemed tame. Claire ran to the shower as soon as we got back. "Phew, I stink!" she said, and she did.

I waited, thinking how I would put it all to her. I was dying to tell her about the kidnapping, but I didn't feel all that clear about how I was going to manage all the rest. Living with Alfie and all. Oh, I was certain about doing it, just not sure about how.

She bounded into the room wearing a blouse and skirt. I couldn't even remember the last time I saw her in a skirt.

"How come?" I asked, pointing, ready to make fun.

She looked down at herself, and I could tell she wasn't ready to joke. As a matter of fact, she scowled. "Yeah, well. . . ." She stood in front of the mirror that hung over her desk and turned around to look at herself over her shoulder. She shook her head. "There's something wrong with me, Les."

"What do you mean, something's wrong with you?" All sorts of things raced through my head.

"There's something wrong with the way I walk! I see myself in store windows and I, well, I see that when I walk I have this wiggle in back, boomtidee boom, side to side, my behind wiggles. Know what I mean? Here, I'll show you, and you tell me the truth."

She walked ahead of me, out to the living room and back.

I didn't know what to say. "Honest, Claire, you just look regular to me." I didn't know what she was talking about.

"I don't look funny? I didn't used to walk that way! I've been noticing. I don't look funny to you? So how come in store windows I can see me sort of . . . rolling in back. It's disgusting!"

I almost laughed but kept it in. I felt maybe a hundred years older, instead of one. "What's disgusting, Claire? What's the matter with you? That's how girls walk. Don't you know that? I mean . . . that's how girls walk." I couldn't believe we were having this conversation. Me, the expert, the Brooklyn Casanova, telling Claire what's what about females.

"Oh, yeah? Well, I hate it, that's all. I'm going to train myself out of it. I'm going to hold myself in somehow. And I don't want to talk about it anymore. Here, I'll show you around, and then we can raid the icebox, since the folks are out, and talk about Alfie."

"So what's upstairs? You said yesterday I gotta see what's up there."

Now when I said that, Claire actually changed color. I swear she got all pink. We were sitting at the kitchen table, ready to dig into some Coke and cold spaghetti. She looked up to the ceiling as if to heaven.

34

"Upstairs are the two most wonderful people in the whole world, and I'm in love with both of them!"

"Oh, Claire! Not again!" I never saw anything like it. For the past year or so, her heart seemed to flop all over the place. If it wasn't Mrs. Curran, her gym teacher, it was Mr. Walinsky, her civics teacher. Love, love, love—it could make you sick.

She frowned at me. "What do you mean, 'not again'? This is for real! My whole life is changed on account of them! Upstairs, there is Lena, who could have been a great pianist, but didn't, because she gave it all up for her son Alex, who is going to be the best violinist in the whole world, Lena says. There's just the two of them. I don't know what happened to the husband. They never say. They're Russian and wonderful and take me to concerts and tell me what books to read and I want to be just like them. I've never met artists before, real ones. Have you?"

"Just Mary the horse." I said.

She paid no attention. "They just opened my eyes, Les. Like I've been asleep or something. You'll see."

Some speech. "Yeah," I said.

Something in the way I said that made her look at me sharply. She knew. "So what about Alfie? Something going on with him?" She swigged the Coke bottle.

"Nothing much. I kidnapped him yesterday."

The Coke sprayed from her mouth like Old Faithful in Yellowstone Park. I got most of it. She coughed, banged the table and, while helping to mop me up, got her voice back and yelled, "WHAT?"

"Really, Claire. Let's have a little reaction here. You

35

take things so calmly." Well, then, of course, I told her everything about the day before, and I was just getting to the part about quitting school and getting a job when I heard her name called from upstairs.

Claire jumped up from the table as if summoned to the Throne by His favorite angel.

"That's Lena!"

She opened the back door just across the room and yelled up, "Lena? You calling me?"

"Yes, my darling. Come up here a moment, will you?"

"I got a friend with me. Okay if I bring him, too?"

"Of course, of course. Him, too."

I couldn't possibly imitate the accent. But it was the voice itself that got me. It was low and rough and sexy all at once, and made you strain for more. I couldn't imagine what was attached to it.

CHAPTER SIX

We climbed the narrow, winding steps. The door was held open by a small woman wearing a turban on her head and nothing else, absolutely naked. I nearly fainted. Then I saw she was wearing one of those dancer outfits, tights and top that look like skin. The trouble was, I was having one of my attacks of self-consciousness, so I could hardly look at her. I was concentrating on control so she would mistake me for the local lifeguard. I didn't know if Claire had told her about me or not.

"I'm Mrs. Lensky, and you will call me Lena." She took my hand and pressed it with both of hers. She wasn't smiling—as if this was too great an occasion for such ordinary politeness. Her lucky day, right? Mrs. Lensky, . . . Lena, was beautiful like a movie star. I was hit by a flash of intense blue from her eyes and had to drop mine. I saw those heavy lids and high cheekbones and that was enough for a while. She was tiny, just about up to my shoulder. Somehow, she didn't seem like a small person.

Claire told her my name and we were invited to sit. We were in the kitchen, same as Claire's downstairs, only what a difference! I never saw plants in a kitchen or paintings on the wall. Everything so bright and unexpected—an embroidered cloth on the table, funny painted dishes piled on it—everything so careless and yet elegant. It all seemed so foreign, better than other kitchens. More cozy.

I heard music from the next room. At first, I thought it was the radio it was so good. Then I realized it must be the son playing the violin, though I wouldn't know a violin from a fishing pole.

"Alex is still practicing," Lena told me, as if everyone knew all about her son Alex. "And I was just doing my exercises."

She swept her hand down her body, and believe me, I followed it every inch of the way. "If I don't exercise every day, I feel so bad," she said. "Don't you find it so?"

For me, just getting from here to there is exercise enough, and Claire never stops exercising, and yet both of us were nodding our heads and agreeing with her—oh yes, one must exercise. She had that kind of . . . something. Like a force that made you want to watch her and listen to her and say *yes, yes, yes*. Another thing, she talked to us as if we were all the same age.

She lit a cigarette and pulled that thing off her head. Blonde! Wouldn't you know it? Hair short and fine as a little girl's. She laughed, sort of a throaty cackle it was, and said, "And now I must wash my hair. And Claire, my darling girl, that's why I called. I went to look, and no shampoo. Would you do me a big favor? Alex is practicing, and of course, nothing must disturb that. Could you buy me?" No one could resist that tone.

Claire jumped up and was at the door in a flash. "I have some. You can use mine. Here, I'll be right back." She was almost gone when Lena stopped her.

"But what kind do you have? My hair is so miserably thin I must be careful what I use." Her words may have been complaining, but her fingers fluffing it were approving. I could tell.

Claire looked blank. "Gee, I don't know. Just some shampoo."

Lena wagged her finger at her. "It's time you paid attention to these things. Soon you will be a beautiful woman and you must be prepared. What do you think, Lester?"

There was a kind of tease in her voice that embarrassed me and yet flattered me at the same time. Claire had no use for that kind of talk at all. "Oh, Lena!" she said. She tugged the door open. "Well, I'll bring it and you'll see."

Lena shrugged and smiled at me through the smoke as if we shared some kind of joke. As if we were old friends. I looked around. "It's nice here," I said, not even close to what I meant.

"Thank you, Lester," Lena said.

The music stopped, and in walked a guy about my own age. As soon as I saw him, I felt the tips of my fingers grow cold.

He was everything that I was not. Well, we both had noses, but the resemblance stopped there. Ever meet anyone who made you feel you stink a little? He moved as if he owned the space around him. He bent over my hand as he shook it and pressed his mother's shoulder as he passed her to swing into a chair opposite me. All those muscles working so smoothly you'd think he moved on wheels. I felt like the town drunk by comparison. He didn't look much like his mother, but he had the same foreign air. He also had the same color hair and eyes, but he was all softer somehow, without those wonderful scooped-out cheekbones of hers. His skin was so smooth and fair I'm sure he didn't have to shave. I think the hairs just fell out on request. When he said, "It's a pleasure, Lester," his voice was deep and perfect just like a radio announcer. What I mean is, I could have killed him.

Claire returned just then, and I watched those two closely. She didn't seem any different with him than with Lena. On her knees with both of them.

So there we were around the table, and Claire told them about what I did the day before, about kidnapping Alfie. I knew she was trying to explain for me, knowing how I was with strangers, but even so, it didn't come out right. Claire made it so light and jokey there was a lot of laughing going on. But I could see Alex and Lena didn't know what to make of it all. They must have thought I was nuts.

They began asking me questions, and pretty soon I was thinking more about Alfie than me, so I was able to talk easily.

I explained how he was changing, why the hospital was bad for him, how important it was to get him out of there before he was all gone. I said, more to Claire than to the others, "I'm going to take Alfie out of that hospital and we're going to live together."

That dropped like a stone on the table. Then Lena broke the silence by saying very gently, "But my dear, what can you be thinking of? You can't be responsible for that sick boy! If he has no mother, then it is up to the father, not you. Now, I remember once when I was touring . . . . I was a concert pianist once, you know. Well, there was a young man. . . ."

Alex interrupted her. "Never mind all that now, Lena." Lena? He calls his mother by her first name? If I did that I'd get such a clop! Lena seemed to spit something at him in another language, but he paid no attention, just went on talking. "Let's find out more what Lester has in mind before discouraging him altogether."

Some sentence. He had to be intelligent, too?

He leaned his elbows on the table and held on to one of his strong stubby fingers. "Let's see the problem we have here. One, I don't suppose you are going to try the kidnapping stunt again, are you?"

I *knew* they thought I was nuts. I shook my head no.

"Well then, so you'll get him out by legitimate means. So, two, where would he go then?"

"Home with me," I said with no trouble at all.

Claire stood up in one of her nervous rushes. "What are you talking about? This is all news to me! You can't bring him home with you, Les. You go to school. You can't just dump Alfie on your mother to take care of. You know your mother doesn't even like you to be with Alfie!"

She was right, I knew. Right away I knew she was right. "I mean home—our own place. My mother doesn't have anything to do with this. Our own place. I'm quitting school and getting a job and then a place to live and then take Alfie out. I can get a job as a messenger or a delivery boy, and Alfie can come around with me. You know he knows his way around. We'll be a team. It'll be okay." I amazed myself. I didn't know I had it all worked out like that. Was it worked out?

I wanted to sound strong and assured like Alex with his big sentences, but I could hear my voice go up about an octave. I tried to think of what it was like riding Mary. All that smooth, strong power.

"Quitting school!" Claire said as if I just said I was going to jump off a bridge.

Lena's look warmed my toes. "You would do that for this friend of yours? You care about him that much? Sacrificing yourself for someone else doesn't work, my dear. I know." For an instant those wonderful eyes rested on her son.

"Mother!" No first name this time. Was he annoyed because she was always bringing herself into the conversation, or what?

"No, no, my darling. I didn't mean you," said Lena, and then again said something in that foreign language. This time they both laughed. Alex said, "Quitting sounds pretty good to me. Could I move in with you, too?" He said that to me but was looking at Lena. They really were the oddest mother and son I ever met. There was some kind of game going on.

Lena asked the same question: Did I care enough for Alfie to do that?

I didn't like that question. It made me feel all mixed up. Sure I was ready to quit school for him. What was the sacrifice? What was I leaving? For an instant, I let myself think how hard it was, what a struggle. Odd man out all the time. A chill went through me when I thought of the future. So pointless . . . someone like me . . . . I shoved all that away, remembering Alfie sitting there in the hospital just waiting for me to rescue him. He needed me. It was not the caring I knew so much about, but the needing. I knew I could do for him. Who else was there I could say that about? Just thinking of us together seemed to make the chill go away. Again, some weight lifted just as it had in Mrs. Brenner's office. I could do for him and that's not nothing. That's not to be sneezed at.

"Yeah," I said to her, and left it at that. Let her think I was an angel of mercy.

"So when is all this going to happen? When do you plan to take your friend out of that hospital for good?" Alex wanted to know.

Lena stood up. All of a sudden she was like a storm. "Don't be ridiculous. You're talking like a child!" She rapped the table. "This cannot be done. It is not good. Get permission to take your friend out for a day, for a weekend, perhaps. We will help you in any way we can. But I cannot agree with this idea of taking him from where he is cared for."

One minute she was angry, and then the next it was like the sun came out. She spread her arms as if to embrace us all. "And now, my darlings, I must shower. Alex, you haven't finished your practicing. Go. No, no, don't run away." This was to Claire and me, who knew a dismissal when we heard one.

43

And Alex knew an order when he heard one. He excused himself and went into the next room to pick up his violin. Claire and I were at the door ready to leave. "Just a moment, Claire," said Lena. She tucked a book under Claire's arm. "This is something I know you will love."

When we were downstairs once again, it was like we'd returned from another world. I could really see why Claire was under their spell.

She danced around the kitchen. "See? I told you! Aren't they wonderful? And Lena's right, Les, about Alfie. It's sad about him, but you can't do anything. I mean like living with him and taking care of him and all. You're still a kid. What you want to be doing is galloping on Mary!"

She walked me to the station, and I thought things over on the train, getting more depressed by the minute.

As usual, I sat on a seat near the door. Opposite me was a lady and her son, maybe nine or ten years old. The kid was just teasing his mother, anyone could see that. He was banging his heels on the seat under them, looking up at his ma, knowing that he was getting her goat. She told him to stop, over and over, but he paid no nevermind to that. Just kept on banging. Then she gave his ear a little twist, and hissed, "Stop it!" And when that didn't work, she was at the ear again, only harder. Well, now they were both caught up in something. He was not going to stop, and she was going to make him. *Bang, bang* went the heels, and he would look up at her with this wise-guy grin and hum a little tune. That just drove her nuts. "You stop that, you!"

And she would grab that ear and twist it so hard that after a couple of times I thought it would come off in her hand. *Bang, bang,* twist . . . *bang, bang,* twist. The kid wouldn't cry out, I give him that, but you could see he was hurting. But he was also eating up her frenzy, too. They just couldn't leave one another alone. I think the mother could have killed the boy with her bare hands . . . and he was egging her on! Like he was asking her to. Well, maybe it would have ended in bloodshed, but thank God, they had to get off the train. Maybe they finished the job at home. Did they hate one another, or what? There was a tremendous . . . something between them, but what it was puzzled me all the way to my stop. Can people love one another and not be able to stand each other at the same time? I don't know, but that weird scene and my own problems made me want to crawl home, all confidence leaving me like a leaking balloon.

CHAPTER SEVEN

I had a great dream once. I must have been, oh, around ten years old. But I remember it like it was last night. In it, Ma took me to a shoe store to buy me a pair of black high-laced basketball sneakers. All my life I've never been allowed to wear sneakers, just these godawful orthopedic shoes. But there we were in a shoe store buying them, the shoe store man fitting me without a word, just as if I were an ordinary kid. Those sneakers filled me with such joy I couldn't speak, couldn't say a word, couldn't open my mouth when the shoe man asked me if I liked them. I just kept staring at those sneakers on my feet, and the man said to Ma, "The kids these days! You pay good money for these and it doesn't mean a thing to them." Ma just laughed because she knew how I was. She paid the man and we walked out with the box.

In my dream, after everyone went to sleep, I put on my new sneakers and went out of the house, down the elevator to the street. Not a soul was in sight. It was quiet and warm, with no wind at all, the moonlight spilling over everything, so I could see fine.

I began to run. No, not just run. I began to leap. Up

and up I bounded, higher and higher every time I came down, and then up again. I jumped over my apartment house to the other side. Another leap and I was over the school building. Up and over, up and over one building after another. It was like playing leapfrog.

Then I was on a highway. I just followed the white line, leaping and leaping. The moon was full and the highway went on forever over mountains and rivers and all. But every once in a while, I would stop to walk around a city. It was still nighttime, but the streets were full of people. I would just walk around and be one of the crowd. No one could tell about me. I wasn't the local cripple, Mrs. Klopper's spastic boy. No one noticed me, no one knew me. I was just another kid walking around. And I knew in my heart that I could bound away, me and my sneakers, down that highway whenever I wanted. I didn't know anyone. I wasn't tied. No one could hurt me at all. And when I had enough of watching, I found my highway and went on.

That's it. That's all.

On the way home from Claire's, I thought of that dream.

The house was empty when I got there. That was a relief. I could smell the chicken cooking in the oven, so I knew Ma was in the building somewhere, visiting friends.

I went into my room and closed the door. I lay on my bed to think things over. I wanted to plan, to be absolutely clear and sensible about what to do next, to think over what everyone was telling me—Mrs. Brenner, Lena, Claire. Instead, what I saw in my head when I closed my eyes was that grotesque little lady in the wheelchair by the elevator, Miss Pink Bow, all dressed up with no place to go. She must have looked in the mirror to pin the bow just so. That made me groan aloud. Then Lena and Alex jumped into my mind. And the ear twisting mother, she and her son. What they were doing to one another. And my own ma clutching at me—clutching at air. Alfie, turning into a zombie before my eyes, and Claire not really with me on that. I thought of my life ahead, having to cope. It all just welled up and overwhelmed me. What was I, some kind of blotter that has to soak up whatever spills out there? What I wouldn't give for those sneakers now.

I couldn't stay on that bed a minute longer. I had to get out of the house.

The beach always makes me feel better, so I headed for it. I really love living near the ocean. I love the smell and the sound. Sometimes at night I can hear the waves pounding four blocks away. The neighborhood isn't so hot, but the ocean makes up for it.

There weren't many people on the beach. Late Sunday in March isn't exactly the height of the season.

I sat on the sand to watch the ocean. The water looked sluggish and very cold, that funny no-color of winter. There were hardly any waves at all, just a small break of white as they spilled over on the shore. There was a volleyball game nearby, a bunch of kids playing without a net, just horsing around, having a good time. I watched them for a while, since they were a lot livelier than the ocean, but soon lost interest and turned back to the soothing distance.

48

I was just staring out, not focused on anything, just thinking of the kidnapping, when I became aware that a shape had stopped nearby.

The shape said, "Hey! It's you! Lester! It's me!"

The same heavy glasses, same big red cheeks and frizzy hair. Instead of the pink smock, she was wearing a heavy sweat shirt.

"Tillie-Rose!" I was so startled to see her again. I had just been running through the kidnapping scene, and there she was before me. I wasn't too crazy about seeing her just then.

She dropped to her knees in front of me. "Isn't this amazing? I was just thinking of you. I was just thinking and here you are. I never saw you on the beach before."

"You don't know anything about me, Tillie-Rose." The ocean should have turned to ice from my voice. "You really loused me up yesterday."

She sank back on her heels. "Oh, listen. I feel just terrible about that. I really do." She clasped her hands in front of her, straining to be believed. "I didn't know what was going on, I didn't know what to do. I would have helped you if I could. Honest. What were you doing anyhow? Why were you taking Alfred away? What did Mrs. Brenner do to you?"

She was so earnest and anxious, like a little kid trying to make up. "Nothing, Tillie-Rose." The hell with her.

She sat looking at me, pouring sand through her fingers, those big glasses slipping off her nose.

"You live around here?" she asked.

"Couple of blocks over."

"Me, too. On the Av. I come here a lot. I know those

kids over there." She meant the volleyball kids. "Sometimes, like tonight, they call me and ask me to bring stuff, and we have a cookout on the beach. We bring blankets and whatever we can find in the house to cook, like potatoes or onions. Ever have a roasted onion? My father has a butcher shop, so it's easy for me. I can always bring franks." With a butcher for a father no wonder they call her, I thought. But there was no hint of that from her. "We build a fire," she continued, "and sit around. It's real nice. You have cerebral palsy, don't you? You're a spastic. I know that from working at the hospital."

Without a pause, without a break between one thought and another, she asked that. Right out. Most people never . . . .

I nodded yes.

She said, "What's it like?"

Bang, the arrow again. No one had ever asked me point-blank before. I was so startled I forgot I was mad at her.

I answered carefully, "I don't have any control over my muscles. They don't do what I say. I say to my arm, 'Get up there. Lift up in the air,' and see what happens?" I showed her, and as usual, my arm waved around like it couldn't make up its mind. "If I concentrate hard and if I'm calm, I have some control. Some. Same with talking. But if I get upset or tense, it's just beyond me. See?" That wasn't the half of it, but I think she did see.

I suspected she saw a lot and I told her so. She laughed, not understanding me on purpose. "Not me," she said. "Without my glasses I'm as blind as a bat. Here, I'll show you."

She put her glasses on my lap and walked back and forth in front of me, groping the air, purposely stumbling around and tripping herself. Finally, she fell on the sand like a sack, hoping to make me laugh.

I did. "Poor Tillie-Rose. You're worse off than I am."

She sat cross-legged in front of me.

"Do you suffer a lot? I think suffering people have beautiful souls, don't you?"

That really made me laugh. What did I have here?

"What do you mean 'suffer'? Not me. I'm happy as the day is long, kid. Couldn't be better. Not a trouble in the world, and I have to beat the girls off. Well, so long."

I began the struggle to stand. Tillie-Rose said, "Wait. You busy? I mean, you have to go home or what?"

I told her I didn't have to, but that I was ready to.

She stood up. "Back in a sec," she said, and ran over to the volleyball game. She stopped the game and did some talking, and then they all stared back at me. I was the big subject.

Whatever the powwow was about, it didn't take long. Tillie-Rose ran back to me with the message from Olympus. "The kids say it's okay if you eat with us. Whattaya think?"

She was elated with the idea and expected me to be.

"No, thanks," I said. I couldn't stand the look on her face, so I tried to be nicer. "I mean thanks very much, Tillie-Rose. It was nice of you to ask but . . . well, no, thanks."

"Why not? It'll be fun. Hey, c'mon, you'll see. Your mother won't let you or something?"

"No, it's not that." I couldn't really tell her why—just everything in me shrank from the idea. Me, with all those normal kids . . . .

"Well, then, if there's no good reason . . . ." She wasn't making it easy for me at all. She pushed her glasses up with a finger and peered at me. She was a funny, dumpy girl who had loused me up yesterday, but she had something.

She'll never know the fright it gave me to finally say yes. "Here, help me up," I said, reaching for her hand. She may as well learn right away what it's like to be with me. "I have to call home."

I found a telephone and called Ma. It was like a Mother's Day present for her. Never mind the soup was on the stove and she'd be eating alone. Pa always ate out on Sundays. I couldn't have made her happier. The fact that a bunch of "normal" kids invited me to a cookout was a piece of news from heaven. Her questions went on and on until I said, "Ma, they're just kids, relax. It's not President Roosevelt, don't get yourself in an uproar. I'll see you later. So long."

I knew how it was with her, and I didn't want to spoil that bit of pleasure I could give her. But she was making me more nervous than ever. I'm not such a pretty sight when I eat. I don't always hit the target. Sometimes I wind up with more food on my face than on the plate.

I didn't have to worry about that. It was dark before we had gathered the wood. I enjoyed that part a lot, remembering how, once, Alfie and I had spent a whole summer doing that. Tillie-Rose and I walked along the beach searching for driftwood as a pair. The rest were in pairs, too, running after one another, wrestling, tossing sticks back and forth, squealing and showing off.

Finally, we were all gathered in front of a big fire, sharing mickeys done just the way I like them best—all charred on the outside and soft and mealy on the inside, tasting a million times better than regular potatoes cooked in an oven. Tillie-Rose had brought enough franks for an army. Somebody else had brought some bread, plain, white Bond bread. Pickles were passed around, and then one of the kids pulled out a jar of peanut butter. Nothing to drink. I'd been introduced when we sat down, but I was largely ignored, except by Tillie-Rose. We shared her blanket, and she saw to it I had whatever there was to eat.

It was chilly on the beach. My front was warmed by the fire, but my back was freezing. Whatever it was I was afraid of had disappeared. I don't know what I thought was expected of me, but nothing was. I was just there.

After we ate, everyone lay back on the blankets and soon it grew very quiet. Tillie-Rose wrapped us both up, and as we lay close together, I tried not to think of what was going on under those other blankets. I tried not to think but I did, and a trembling started within me at the bone and spread to every corner. "You cold, Les? I can feel you shivering," said Tillie-Rose, so close to me I could feel her breath on my face.

I could only grunt, wanting her to think it was the chill getting me. She's just a kid, I said to myself, grateful for the fact.

"Gee, look at the stars!" said Tillie-Rose, plumping herself away from me. "Aren't they a sight?"

I managed to point out the few I knew. Now that the fire was dying down, the sky was immense, the stars bright enough to touch. What I yearned for was her breath on my face again. As if she read my mind, she turned to me again. I had forgotten what she looked like, what she was. I felt only her friendliness and her liking and the fact that she was female. That blotted out the sky and the stars, and I felt only her breath and her closeness.

"Do you like to kiss?" she asked me then. Do I like to . . . ? Do I like . . . ? I couldn't summon the strength to tell her that I had never . . . that I had never. How could I? Who would? Well, she would. She leaned over me and put her lips on mine and put her hand on my cheek, and kissed me. I felt the fearful, pleasurable surge deep within me. But strongest of all was the joy of touch, her hand, her lips, her closeness.

I held her hand against my face and pulled away. "Thanks, Tillie-Rose," I said, glad it was dark.

"Do you have a girl friend? I mean, do you like someone else?" What an astonishing girl!

There I was, so unexpectedly happy, a dream of mine coming true. I was practically alone with a girl who seemed to like me. Never mind that she was too young, awkward, funny looking or anything else. She liked me. Tillie-Rose asked a simple question about a girl friend, and suddenly, as if a gong struck, Claire leaped to mind. I saw her tall, bony body draped in a chair as graceful as a cat, looking at me with those gray eyes, laughing

54

that great laugh of hers. I saw her and I knew I loved her. I knew why it mattered to me how she was with Alex. She was my old friend who, out of the blue, changed from that person into this new one whom I knew I loved.

"Yes, I do," I said. "I like you Tillie-Rose. This was wonderful tonight and I like you. I just realized when you asked me that I like someone else, too. A lot."

"Why that's the most romantic thing I ever heard! You mean you just now found out that you love her? Does she love you back? What's her name?"

"Her name is Claire and she doesn't know at all. We're old friends."

"Oh . . . wow!" Tillie-Rose sat up to lean on her elbow. "That's okay. I don't mind. I didn't expect you to . . . I mean, we can still be friends and all. You haven't even told me yet what you were doing with Alfie yesterday. We'll see each other again, right? No reason not to, right?"

There wasn't any reason in the world. But just then I was ready to be alone so I could think about my discovery. It was as if I had found a secret treasure I could spread out and gloat over any time I wanted. It was better than finding a treasure. This was inside me where it couldn't be lost and was mine entirely. What Claire felt for me didn't matter at all at that moment. I didn't want or expect anything at all. In that one single moment, I felt my whole life had changed. I was connected with it in a new way.

CHAPTER EIGHT

Why is it, I wonder, that when I'm feeling good I can never remember what it's like to feel bad. And the other way around, too. I knew I felt just awful yesterday just before the beach and Tillie-Rose, but that was like remembering another person. That person didn't know what I knew.

"I'm in love!" I said to the silly face in the bathroom mirror that morning, getting ready for school. "I'm in love with Claire." If only I could sing or hop around or hug myself. I stuck out my tongue and licked the mirror. Being "in love" was so different from loving. "So this is what it's all about," I said to my toothbrush. I wanted to write a thank-you note to Claire. It was quite enough; I couldn't handle a thing more, not another drop.

Ma saw it right away at breakfast. "Someone's feeling happy this morning," she said. Sitting across from me at the table, even she, in her old bathrobe, hair uncombed, creased face, looked good to me.

"And someone looks real nice this morning," I told her.

"Oh, you!" she flapped her hand at that and her nose

got all pink. "What was I, asleep in my chair when you got home? Why didn't you wake me up? Was it late? You know I can't sleep a wink until you're home. Must have been some time at the beach last night, mmmmmh? So?" The question lady.

"Yeah, I had a real nice time, Ma. Good-by, gotta go, the bus is waiting." I got up and kissed her cheek and got out of there. I couldn't talk to her about it. I'd get to feel all tangled inside, and I wasn't going to have any of that with the wonderful bubble inside me.

Even my talk with the principal of my school, Mr. Morgan, didn't pop the bubble. I get to leave class a few minutes before the bell so I can make my way to the next without dealing with the crowd. He passed me in the hall and told me to come see him.

"You're a smart boy, Lester," he told me, getting out my folder from the files. "You're not working, but you're smart enough. What's the matter? Anything on your mind? Anything wrong at home?"

"Not a thing, Mr. Morgan."

"If I thought you could take the struggle, I could get you into a college. There are scholarships for boys like you. We could do it, but you'd have to show me you're interested."

We had a couple of legal blinds and a few polios in the school, but for the past two years, since I entered, I had the special honor of being the only cerebral palsy. I was the star—like I was representing them all in the Lame Olympics and they were counting on me to win.

So I was "smart," eh? Well, that's his opinion. He didn't know my future was all settled. I woke up with it all laid out for me. I didn't know love cleared the head. I didn't feel mixed-up at all any more. I'll show them. I'll show Mrs. Brenner and Lena. Claire will be proud. I'll show them all. I was going to look for a job that very afternoon. I'd start with anything, maybe a delivery boy, and work myself up. I'd find a little place to live and get Alfie, and he would come around with me and help. Maybe we could make a real business of it someday. Sure. "Klopper and Burt, Partners." Sure. Why not?

Some days everything goes your way. Right after school, I started looking for a job, and right off the bat, I got one. Just like that.

I hit Apatow's drugstore first thing. It's right on the corner and he knows me. He was in back, sitting on his stool pouring pills from one bottle to another. I had never been back there. From floor to ceiling, all I saw were boxes and bottles.

"A job, Lester? You want to work *here*?" Mr. Apatow's eyes went blank for a moment. His hair was parted just above one ear so the few strands could cover the top of his head, but there was always a hank hanging down to his shoulder. He smoothed this piece into place, and then buttoned his white jacket. He sure was taking his time thinking things over.

Then he said carefully, "What about your schooling? You must be busy with schoolwork. Soon a graduate."

I told him not to worry about that. I didn't want to explain just then about working with my friend Alfie. I just told him I had to help out at home. Everybody likes that idea.

He shook his head and did that clicking noise with

the tongue that means too bad. "That's no good, Lester, quitting school. For that you'll be sorry one day." He looked me up and down. "A boy like you . . . ." He stopped and started again. "A boy like you needs all the education he can get."

People get all dreamy about education. They think it's the answer to everything. Apatow wouldn't have the faintest idea of what a battle it would be for me. I told him I was going to get a job, no matter what.

He looked at the bottle of pills in his hand for a moment and then slowly put it down on the counter. He sighed. He slid off the stool and stood up. "Tell you what," he said, "I'll put you to work here a couple of days, and we'll see how it works out. But . . . ." He made a stop sign with his hand. "But don't quit school for a while. Try it out a few days *after* school, and then see. If it works out, it works out. If not, nothing lost. No bridges burned. Heh, heh."

Something in there must have been a joke, but I didn't get it. Nevertheless, I laughed and agreed like a madman. Wow, a job right off, and so easy! I didn't mind about the after school part as a start. It would only be until he saw how good I was.

"When do you want to start?" Mr. Apatow asked. "How about next week. Say, Monday?"

"I'm ready right now, Mr. Apatow. Got any deliveries for me?" I wanted to show him he had a willing worker here.

He had a few he was going to drop off himself on his way home to supper. As he handed me two packages, the first of my troubles with that job started. I hadn't thought. I couldn't carry stuff with my hands and walk at the same time. Apatow saw the problem right away. He reached under the counter and brought out a shopping bag for the packages. That I could handle.

I'm not what you could call a fast walker. Slow and steady may win the race but, slow and unsteady can still make deliveries. I knew the neighborhood, and the two deliveries were for around there. It took me a little while, to put it mildly, and by the time I got back to the store, Mr. Apatow was closing for the supper hour. We agreed that I could come right after school the next day, and I went home mighty pleased with myself.

I couldn't wait to call Claire, to hear that husky voice again with my new ears. I wanted to tell her about the job, though I wouldn't go into what it was for. I wanted to tell her about the wild coincidence of meeting Tillie-Rose at the beach after, and the cookout. But the rest . . . oh, the rest—the kiss, my discovery, my Claire!—I would keep to myself for awhile.

I telephoned the minute I got home. She was all over me with questions and teasing. For the first time in ages, she had to say "What? What?" when I talked. I wanted to sound extra smooth and easy, so, of course, I loused myself up and did the opposite. I could hardly get the words out. That kind of thing could give love a bad name.

The big thing for me was that she said she'd stop by Saturday morning. I didn't even have to ask. She said she wanted me to meet some great new friend of hers who lived near me.

"A boyfriend?" I croaked. I was trying to sound casual,

and instead it was as if someone had slipped a tray of ice cubes down my fly.

"Female, you nut. Always thinking of sex!" she said scornfully, and then we hung up. I wanted to kiss the mouthpiece but I couldn't stand being a total idiot.

It was on the third day of work that disaster struck. I was reading in the back room, the bottle room, I called it. I was sitting on the chair Mr. Apatow had for me back there, waiting for him to finish some prescriptions so I could deliver. It was really nice back there and I appreciated that Apatow let me read instead of waiting on customers or helping behind the fountain. I just couldn't do the fountain work. The day before, some ladies had come in. I went over and asked them if I could help. They acted like I was deaf *and* stupid. They smiled a lot and spoke loudly and said they would find what they wanted themselves. Then, when they went to pay Apatow, I could see them leaning over the counter and talking and looking over their shoulders at me and talking some more. It was after they left that Mr. Apatow brought in the chair for me to sit on out back. Okay by me.

Well, there I was, alone in the room, and it occurred to me that I could make myself useful instead of reading. Mr. Apatow was out front waiting on a customer, and I was sure he would like it if I cleaned up a bit for him. I found the broom and the dust pan and began to sweep. I know how it's done. God knows I've seen my mother do it often enough. Usually when I'm holding on to something, I have more control. And I did. I thought I was doing a good job. Then, I don't know, I breathed, I blinked, something, and my foot caught, and I tripped. I put my arm out to steady myself and pulled down a whole shelf of bottles with me as I fell. The broom fell the other way and swept off some bottles and boxes on the other side. We were pretty thorough, that broom and I. A clean sweep you might say.

It was awful. I wasn't hurt, but it was awful. Mr. Apatow was so nice about it—considering. But, of course, that was the end of the job.

I spent the rest of the week after school hunting. In one store and out the other. No one needed help. Or they didn't after taking a look at me. I stuck it out though; I kept looking.

Friday afternoon it was pouring. I was walking along the avenue a couple of blocks over, keeping close to the store windows so the rain wouldn't get at me so much. I was headed for the five-and-ten thinking maybe I could help out in the storeroom.

I heard my name called out and there was Tillie-Rose standing out in the rain a few stores away, holding a mop and grinning at me.

I nearly burst out laughing at the sight of her. She looked so funny standing there in the rain, such a rolypoly, with her glasses slipping down her nose and her hair like the mop she was holding. A long white apron covered her almost to her shoes.

"Gosh, am I glad to see you!" she said. "This is my father's store. Come on inside, out of the wet."

I followed her into the butcher shop, holding my

breath against the smell of blood and chicken feathers and I didn't even like to think what else.

The store was crowded. The man behind the counter wearing a straw hat and a blood-stained apron could only have been her father. Same fat cheeks, same round body, only he had a great black mustache like a walrus. There may have been some lips under it, but I couldn't see them. He had a mouth, though. He pointed a long, gleaming knife at his daughter. "So, *nu?* Tillie, get a move on. The orders are piling up. Finish the back, already, and get busy on the orders." His loud, good-natured laugh rose above the din of the customers. He winked at the one he was waiting on. "What can I do with my beautiful good-for-nothing of a daughter, eh, Mrs. Minder? A jewel I have. A lazy jewel, but she takes care of me like nobody's business."

"I'll get to the orders later, Poppa. I have company now. See ya." She raised her mop to him and waved to me to follow her. We trooped across the sawdust floor and around the customers to the back.

CHAPTER NINE

I followed her down a long hallway and into a large room that was like a kitchen, and then again not. I mean it had a stove and icebox and cups and plates on open shelves, along with boxes and cans of things to eat. But it also had an easy chair in a corner and lamps and a radio, which made it like a living room, too.

"We live back here," she said. I could see that.

"Want something?" She opened the icebox and bent over, looking in. "Cream soda? Root beer? Hey, sit down."

We settled at the big round table in the middle of the room.

We smiled at one another. Maybe she was remembering the kiss, too.

"Tillie-Rose, Tillie-Rose. What's your last name? I don't even know your name."

"Tillie-Rose Bloom," she said, just as if it were ordinary.

I nearly choked. "Say, that's wonderful. There's a girl in my class, her name is Rosebud Gesundheit. That's almost as good as yours."

"Yeah, and there's a boy I know, his name is Jerry Titz. Get it? Titz. How do you like that?" She giggled. "What's yours?"

"Lester Klopper."

A cat out of nowhere jumped on my lap, making me spill my root beer. Another walked across the cracked linoleum and jumped on the big chair in the corner. Tillie-Rose gathered them both up in her arms and dumped them out the back door.

She wiped up the root beer. "Where's your mother?" I asked.

"No mother. Me and my poppa, we get along okay. There's just the two of us, and we get along okay. He was only kidding when he called me lazy." While she talked to me, she was putting meat scraps in dishes and setting them outside the door. "Lots of strays live off my poppa," she said.

I asked about her mother, whether she was dead or divorced, or what. Tillie-Rose rested her cheeks against her fists and told me some story. She must have told it or maybe just thought about it a lot because it came out so pat. I mean, it wasn't like she was telling me a family secret or anything. It was more like she was telling me a movie plot she had seen the night before. For all I knew it was.

Her mother, as a girl in Poland, had a boyfriend she couldn't marry because he had aged parents to take care of. That's how it was in the old days, she told me. Then her parents married her off to a man who was free and had a good trade, a butcher, Tillie-Rose's father. They came to this country, and six months after Tillie-

Rose was born, the old boyfriend came after her, free to marry. "So she ran off with him," said Tillie-Rose.

"And left you?" I said, trying to keep the shock from my voice. I didn't know mothers could do that.

"That's the only way my father would let her divorce him. She had to leave me behind. Don't you think that's a romantic story?" Her eyes said nothing behind those glasses.

She changed the subject. "Hey, you never told me what you were doing with Alfie last Sunday. Tell me. What?"

She took it all in, leaning on her elbows across from me at that wooden table, listening without moving as if we had all the time in the world. She had a way of looking at you as you spoke, as if what you said really mattered to her. For a change, I didn't have to worry how I sounded, and the less I worry, the better it goes. It felt like I was pouring cream, it all came out so easy. I began with the old days, how Alfie was my first and best friend and what he was like then and how the hospital had changed him and how I was just overrun by the idea of taking him out of there last week. I told her I was going to do that. "This time legal," I said. Alfie was going to live with me as soon as I got a job, some money and a place.

When I was done, she looked at me like I was little Lord Jesus himself.

"That's beautiful, Les. That's the most beautiful thing I ever heard. I don't know how you're going to do it, but I just want you to know what I think."

Then the hands were clasped under her chin in that

special prayer way of hers. "You've got to let me help. This time I'm going to help. For one thing I can get you a job right here. I can tell my poppa I can't take care of the house and help out in the store, too. I'll tell him he's right, I'm lazy. I'll tell him anything. Poppa does what I want."

I was dumbfounded at my luck. A job!

She clapped her hand to her forehead as if struck. "Oh! There's something else." She stopped whatever it was she was going to tell me as if she was having second thoughts. I think she was sorry she mentioned it. Then she changed her mind again. "Yes, yes, it will be terrific. You'll see. Come on, Les, there's something I want to show you."

We went out her back door and stepped into a tiny backyard that was filled mainly with cats, garbage pails and broken pieces of cement. The most cheerful things were the lines of laundry hanging from the windows of the apartment building opposite. It seemed so close I could have jumped into the underwear hanging there. "It's down here in the basement, what I want to show you. Watch the steps."

It was pitch black in the basement. If there were windows, time and the soot from the coal bin had covered them over like blinders. We stood for a moment to get used to the darkness. Tillie-Rose reached over to a shelf and lit a candle. Lucky for me Tillie-Rose wasn't a fast mover. I followed the gleam, trying to avoid the easy stumble. She held the candle so I could see what my foot was stepping on. It was like a cave in there. We walked in the dark until we came to what looked like a

67

wall, a wooden wall. I couldn't imagine what she had to show me. In that place, it could have been a couple of hibernating bears.

"Ready?" she asked me.

"I guess so."

"Wait a minute. Stay out here until I call you."

No one would have noticed there was a door there. She slipped inside, leaving me blind. What was I in for?

She called and I entered.

I stood absolutely amazed. I was in a circus tent. Dozens of candles lit a room full of color. Sheets draped the ceiling and walls, and hanging here and there and all over were the queerest things I've ever seen in a room— old hats, streamers from kids' parties, pieces of driftwood and shells, old soup cans painted up with faces or flowers and more and more and more. To top it all, hanging from the ceiling was an enormous birdlike thing made of thick paper all painted up with feathers stuck here and there. Amazing. I couldn't take it all in at once. It was such a wonderful jumble of things to look at. The whole crazy room filled me with a gush of pleasure. I couldn't stop smiling.

"You do this?" Maybe the silliest question of my life. I couldn't help marveling that this pudgy, funny kid had it in her.

She didn't bother answering that. She said, "I come here to hide out. You know, to be alone. I bring a book, or my drawing, something to eat." There was a mattress on the floor piled with pillows. "Sometimes I sleep." She looked around the room with satisfied eyes. "I've been

68

wanting to show this to someone. I've been wanting to, but it had to be right. You know?"

I wandered around, getting a closer look at all there was to see. I noticed here and there some drawings pinned to the sheets—queer dark shapes and violent jets of color. I didn't know what to make of them, I liked them, but they disturbed me.

"You're a talented person, Tillie-Rose. You know that? The room, the drawings and all."

"You really think so? You telling the truth?" She took a step closer and clasped my arms. Something had lit those cheeks and eyes. "Well, have I got something to tell you! Les, upstairs I had the most wonderful idea! You don't have to wait with Alfie, to get him out. He can stay here, right here in this room until you get a place of your own. I'll take care of him just fine, and you can visit him any time you want. Isn't this just perfect? You can take him out for good and all, right now!"

Whoa, whoa. I backed away. "Hey, wait a minute, Tillie-Rose. Wait a damn minute. I can't let you. . . ."

"No, no, don't worry about me. I can take care of him, maybe even better than you can. I had experience in the hospital and I like taking care. Really I do."

I took another step away. I wanted to say fifty things at once. "I appreciate this and all, but I'm not taking Alfie out to put him here! Oh, don't get me wrong, it's a wonderful place. But for God's sake, Tillie-Rose, it's dark here, for one thing. And underground . . . and I don't know, it's not right—him here and me someplace else, it's not what I meant." I looked around to sit. The nerve of her! He's *my* friend. I couldn't begin to tell her how wrong the whole thing was. How could she possibly think it was okay?

I was glad for the mattress on the floor. She could see how upset I was, how her great plan backfired. She was crushed. I'm a terrible coward when it comes to hurting people's feelings. Just to ease things up a bit so she wouldn't look at me like that, I said, "I know what. Let's get my friend Claire in on this, okay? I want you two to meet, anyway."

"Claire? Oh. The one who . . . ? Oh, sure! I'd love to meet her. She know about you and her yet? I mean, did you tell her yet about how you feel?"

"Not yet. But I'm seeing her tomorrow. Maybe I'll bring her over. Yeah. Maybe I'll tell her tomorrow." I suddenly needed to. There were so many flies buzzing around my head, like what am I doing? Can I really handle all this? How would it be after? Too many to swat. I needed to get back to that wonderful bubble. Maybe telling would do it.

When we got back to her kitchen, I asked about me working there. "Did you mean it, Tillie-Rose?"

She said sure she meant it and that I could deliver orders around the neighborhood. That was fine with me.

"Do you think there's a chance of it working into a full-time job? It's a real job I'm looking for, you know." No sooner was that out of my mouth than I realized what I was asking. This was a butcher shop, for Chrissake. A butcher shop with knives and all. I couldn't do that in a million years. Customers would have a slice of Lester along with their steaks.

"Forget it, Tillie-Rose. I'll see you sometime tomorrow. We'll work something out about Alfie. At least we can plan a weekend visit, okay?"

I just didn't know what I was going to do about finding a full-time job. I was kidding about the flies. What was buzzing around my head were buzzards.

CHAPTER TEN

Ma said, "Why are you so nervous this morning?"

I said, "No reason," and then the doorbell rang and there was Claire.

Ma shot me a look that asked about ten of her questions at once. What's going on here? What's up? My son is nervous and then Claire comes? Can it be what I'm thinking?

She gave me a look and then welcomed Claire like a long lost daughter. My poor, hopeful ma.

"Hello, stranger. My, my, it's good to see you again! Lester tells me you like your new house, may you live in it and be well. Look at her, shooting up like a regular beanpole, every time more inches. You're looking, ah . . . good. Isn't she, Lester? Come in, come in."

"Hi, Mrs. Klopper. Nice to see you again. Hi, Les. Got a drink of water for me? I ran all the way from the station."

She looked it. I knew why Ma had that hesitation in her voice when she said how good Claire looked. Dirty white shorts, a T-shirt and an old purple-and-gold school team jacket was not Ma's idea of snappy dressing.

But to me, seeing her for the first time since my big discovery, I felt as if I were seeing a new person. Everything she did, every movement, was absorbing to me: Her long stride into the kitchen seemed elegant; her neck as she drank, suddenly delicate; her large, capable hand grasping the glass, the perfect size; her thin, bony body standing at the sink, full of grace. I could have watched her drink that water for hours.

She put down the glass and grinned at me. "Hey, Les, what do you say we take a walk, go past my old house, see who's around, okay? Also, I want you to meet this new friend of mine, Jean. She's just a couple of blocks from here. Okay?"

"Sure. And after, we'll go see Tillie-Rose. The one I told you about?"

She laughed and poked me. "Oh, sure, the funny face. The fat girl from the hospital. Well, let's go. So long, Mrs. Klopper."

"She's not all that funny looking," I said to her back. She was already pushing the elevator button before I was out the door.

It was one of those spring days where you're hot in the sun and chilly in the shade, and everywhere you look seems washed clean. Claire threw back her head and stretched her long neck to sniff the sharp breeze. "Mmmmmm, I smell the ocean. God, I miss that!"

Just hearing her say that set me up for the day. I loved hearing anything that connected her with me, old times and the neighborhood.

We didn't say much, walking down the block. She was busy looking around and waving hi to people. Once in a while, she'd point out something, as if surprised it was still standing after a whole month.

"Hey, there's the old schoolyard."

"Hey, there's my old apartment house." What did she think? It would all disappear when she left? Then she grabbed my hand and turned me around so that we were heading for a side street. "Let's go see Jean. She's new on my team at school. Maybe she'd like to mooch around with us. You'll like her, Romeo, because she's pretty."

That was the girl Claire went to see with her friend Blanchie last week, when she should have been kidnapping Alfie with me. I wondered if Alfie would have been with us that very minute if she had.

Jean Persico lived a few blocks away on Brighton 10th. All the apartment houses look alike in my neighborhood, but there's an altogether different smell to each. Hers smelled of onions and old carpet.

Claire rang the bell, and when the girl opened the door I could see right away she wished she hadn't. The smile died on her face when she saw us, and instead of opening the door for us to come in, she slipped outside and closed it behind her. For a big girl, she was a quick mover. If she had eyes in her head, I didn't see them because they were either caught by something down the hall or fixed on Claire's knees. I didn't care, because who needs eyes when I had that absolutely wonderful hair to look at, like staring into the sun.

Claire said, "Hiya, Jean. This is my friend Les I told you about. We were just walking around. Wanna come?" She knew something was up because she had that care-

74

ful tone of hers I knew so well. At a moment's notice it could turn into a block of ice.

Then, right there in that dark hallway, I saw the most embarrassing embarrassed person that ever lived. It's terrible for me to watch someone squirm like that. It makes me want to jump into bed and pull the covers over my head. The poor girl was trying to tell Claire . . . something, but what? She couldn't come for a walk, couldn't see her again, couldn't be with her. But why? I actually heard her say her mother said so. Her mother said she didn't want her to be friends with Claire any more. All this mumbled in such a nicey-nice way it was hard to make out.

"What? What do you mean? Your *mother* said that? Come on, Jean, I can't hear you. I can't *believe* this! What are you telling me about your *mother*, for cryin' out loud!"

Just then, Jean's name was called from inside that door. You never saw such relief. "I have to go!" she whispered. Claire grabbed Jean's skirt. "Not yet, you don't! Who cares about seeing you! But I want to know. . . ."

"Who is it, Precious?" And then, before Claire finished telling Jean off, Mama was at the door to see who Precious was talking to.

Mama didn't have any trouble with her eyes. One look at Claire and all expression left them. They stared at us without a blink, just the way a frog stares at a rock. I wasn't introduced, which was okay with me since I had already met a frog. She nodded at Claire, and her mouth went into one of the false smiles that wouldn't fool a fool. "Could I see you a moment, Jean?" she said to her daughter without taking her eyes from us. At last I thought I saw something in them . . . a bit of fear maybe, certainly a kind of curiosity.

Then Claire spoke up. "Wait a minute, Mrs. Persico. Jean says she's not supposed to be friends with me anymore. I mean she says *you* said. That's what you said? That's what you meant?"

"Don't take that tone with me, young lady! I don't have to stand here and answer questions. Say good-by to these people, Jean."

Claire put her foot in the door to stop it from being closed in our faces. "Wait a minute. This is crazy! What's going on here? Why can't I see Jean? Why can't I see you, Jean?"

Claire was loud, and this really got a rise from Jean's mother. This time she let herself go. The door was held open, the other hand pushed her daughter behind her, protecting her from the enemy. She spoke to Claire as if she smelled rotten, the words falling from those lips like they were stones to throw. "I'll tell you why, young lady. I know what you are. I have eyes. I could see how you were with your so-called friend Blanche when you were here. I saw you mushing it up on the couch. Well, I'll tell you one thing. I'm not going to have my daughter mixed up in any unhealthy thing like that. You heard me. Unhealthy. Shame!"

The door slammed and we were left staring at it.

At the end of my block is a sandy, empty stretch of

stones and weeds and bushes. Ma never used to let me go there when I was younger because I would always trip in the holes or over stones. But for a long time now, it's been one of my favorite places. Alfie and I used to go there when we were collecting bugs. It's a good place to talk.

We headed for the old log where the black remains of zillions of cookout fires were still around.

I sat and waited while she poked some charred wood with the toe of her sneaker. I was having trouble with my breath. I had to strain to hear her. In a kind of wondering, flat voice, she said, "She asked me over, and I said could I bring Blanchie because I knew they would like each other, and so we both went. We were in the living room, see, just sitting around. Me and Blanchie were on the couch, and Blanchie puts her feet up and lies down with her head in my lap. I knew she had a headache and didn't feel so hot. Can you see it? Me and Blanchie on the couch with her head in my lap?"

She wasn't looking at me, she was looking at a picture inside her head.

"So that . . . that woman, that Mrs. Persico, was in and out, Jean's mother. She'd smile as she passed through, but not so much, not so friendly, I noticed right away. But who cares, right? I was stroking Blanchie's head, I guess, not thinking about it, just stroking and talking, and Mrs. Persico in and out."

She stopped, and dug some more with her toe.

"Go on, so what?" I was waiting for the mushy part.

She spread her palms. She almost yelled. "Then nothing. That's it! Then nothing. Then the three of us went for baseball practice, that's what then. That's what's 'unhealthy'! That's what's 'shame.'"

We stared at one another. "What's she mean then?" I asked, though I knew very well.

She began to nod her head and said, "I see now. I see. It all fits. Yop, that's it." She wasn't talking to me. She sat down next to me on the log and said, "I just thought of something, Les. It fits. There's more to this. Listen to this. Blanchie told me, oh, weeks ago, something, and we just sort of laughed about it. Know what she told me? Mr. Rubin, our English teacher, called her in to talk about some composition she had handed in. You know how much I love him. He's the most wonderful man in the whole world, and when he looks at me, I could just die. And after, after they talked about her work, she said he asked some funny questions about me. Like, do I have any boyfriends? Do I ever dress up? Do I like girl things? Stuff like that. About me. We just didn't know what to think. So we laughed."

She jumped up, and in one single motion, kicked a stone and sent it sailing. The smoothness of that motion, the beauty of all those easy connections, made my chest hurt. She had no idea how lovely she looked, so hurt and so graceful.

Still looking after the stone, she said, "Those two have it in their heads that I'm some kind of queer. What do you think of that!"

What she wanted from me I was in no way able to give. I knew what "queers" were, but I never could figure out exactly what they *did*. To think of Claire that way just left me blank.

She lifted her arms and then clapped them down against her body in a way I've seen very old people do when they give up. She was trying not to cry. "What bothers me so much right now is that I've been in Mr. Rubin's class a long time now. I see him after class every chance I get. I practically follow him around. He knows me. Knows me! So how could he think that? That lady Mrs. Persico—she doesn't know me. But he does. So how could he think that? It makes me feel that if he could think that, then nobody can know anything about anybody. You know what I mean? Or else . . . ."

She broke off and bit her lip and sat down beside me and touched my knee. "Or else, Les, maybe he's right. Maybe they are both right. I have to think about that. Maybe those two people see something about me, *know* something. After all, they're grown-up, adult people, they should know about things like that."

I had to cry out, "Well, don't *you* know, for Chrissake? Don't you know about yourself?"

She positively blazed at me. "No, I don't! No, I don't know! Maybe I should, but I don't."

All the tough, cool Claire was gone. She quieted down, and like a little kid she hung on to my hand and said, "Listen, Les, I hear the girls talking. You know, all about boys and how far to go and how exciting this one is and wow, when he puts his hand here, or should I let him put his hand there—all that stuff. Well, I feel so outside of things that way. I just haven't had any . . . you know . . . ." She waved her hand helplessly to show me all that steamy world of sex out there still closed to her, still a mystery. It struck me how . . . young she was. For all her years and for all her inches, she just wasn't there yet. My Sleeping Beauty.

"It's true, it's true," she wailed. "I fall for all kinds of people. It doesn't seem to matter what they are. I mean, whether they're men or women. I can't help it if I love my gym teacher. She's so beautiful and wonderful. And same with my friends—Blanchie, Dimpie, Franny . . . I love them. I do. Does that make me queer? There's other people too—Lena and Alex and Mr. Rubin and Mr. Walinsky, who makes me shiver when he looks at me, and old Mrs. Giambetti up the street who sings Italian to me. Does that mean anything? I thought everyone was like that."

And just when I was trying to think of what to say to all that, some kids ran by, saw us and stopped. Not so much kids—maybe twelve or thirteen year olds, and rough looking. That was one of the troubles with the lot. Some of the Sheepshead Bay gangs used it, and you had to be careful. There were three of them—ragged sweaters, torn pants, each wearing a beanie hat cut down from a man's fedora with crazy buttons sewed on them. They were kids, but they scared me plenty.

They stood with their feet apart, hands on hips or else tossing a rock up in the air and staring at us. I don't mind telling you I started to shake. Wrestling isn't my best sport.

"Hey, gimpy, who's the girl friend?" one of them asked. This was a big joke to the others.

"Yeah," said the one with the rock, looking at Claire in an awful way. Up and down his eyes went, taking her all in. "What can a gimp do with her? Should we show him?"

At that, Claire jumped up, and I don't know how she managed so fast, but she had a heavy stick in her hands that would have smacked right down on the guy's beanie if he hadn't jumped away. All three of them started to run, she was so fierce swinging away with that stick, like Babe Ruth up at bat.

As soon as they began to run, something unlocked in my own legs. I don't know what was in my head, but I stumbled after them. It wasn't anything I willed, I was just after them. What did I think I was going to do, beat them up? Catch them and force them to their knees until they begged for mercy? I couldn't even keep my balance. My breath twisted, my feet twisted and I was down.

From a safe distance, one of the boys yelled back, "All that meat and noooo potatoes."

Claire stood there shaking that stick, brave and furious. One minute she was a scared little girl and the next an Amazon! And people wanted to put a label on her, pin her down! She didn't fit into any box I knew of. It only took an instant as I watched her shaking that stick, but I thought to myself I might as well have fallen in love with a seagull. What she was and what she needed was beyond me.

She threw the stick after them and yelled, "UN-HEALTHYYYYY!!"

I yelled after them, "SHAME!"

And so that part ended for us in a laugh. She gave me a hand up and I didn't let go of it. I couldn't help myself. I had to tell her, no matter what.

"I love you, Claire!" Finally, finally, it was out.

"You betcha, Les. I love you, too," she said.

Not the same thing at all.

CHAPTER ELEVEN

Introducing Claire to Tillie-Rose was like introducing the tree to a puppy. Claire, tall and skinny, was stiff, almost rooted to the ground, while pudgy little Tillie-Rose was all push-push and gabble-gabble. She all but wagged her tail. Neither of them was acting right, I mean like themselves. One part of me watched all this like a play, and another part felt terrible. I wanted so much for them to like one another. Maybe that was the trouble; they knew how anxious I was.

It was a beautiful day, the sun warm and the air cool. I sniffed the seaweed breeze coming off the ocean. Spring was coming, no mistake. The trolley clacked by, and I could see people standing on the running board, riding along outside. That was one sure sign of good weather. On a Saturday afternoon there were plenty of people walking the streets. The men were in shirt sleeves, their jackets slung over one shoulder and their ties loosened. The women were without the kerchiefs on their heads, their bright dresses another sure announcement of spring. I could always tell the change of season more by the clothes people wore than by what the grass and trees were doing. There in Brooklyn by the beach, what trees? Only tree I could see was Claire, letting herself be sniffed by Tillie-Rose.

"Let's show Claire your room," I said, to break the awkwardness. After all, Tillie-Rose had offered the room for Alfie, and we had agreed to ask Claire about it. When I said that, she shot me a look that would have drawn blood if it had had teeth.

"Nah, some other time. Claire doesn't want to see some old room."

Well, that I couldn't figure out at all. What had gotten into Tillie-Rose all of a sudden?

"Sure I'd like to see it," said Claire, still stand-offish. She didn't have an idea in the world what she was in for.

It was a complete surprise to her, as I knew it would be. After standing there in the candlelight for a moment to take it all in, she went wild. The room did it. Whatever was holding her back, whatever was making her afraid to be herself, just disappeared. She danced around that small room, beside herself with delight. One of the old-fashioned straw hats hanging from the sheets went on her head, and the room was filled with her squeals. "Hey, did you do these?" She had stopped in front of one of Tillie-Rose's dark drawings. It looked to me like some kind of queer bird smashing an egg against a monster. Phew. "I love pictures that make me laugh," said Claire. She took one of the painted soup cans from the wall and squinted at Tillie-Rose through it, as if looking through a telescope. "Aha! Ladies and gentlemen, I draw your attention to a new star in the heavens.

84

A gen-u-wine Rose-in-bloom, called from henceforth on, 'Silly-Tillie, the Artist!' " Claire took off the old hat and clapped it on Tillie-Rose's head. "Tah-dah!" She shook Tillie-Rose by the shoulders. "Tillie-Rose, Silly-Tillie, this is a perfect room. I love it! You're an honest-to-God wonder to do this!"

Now everything was reverse. It was Tillie-Rose who quieted, and it was Claire who frisked around.

Behind those thick glasses, Tillie-Rose's button eyes shone. She clasped her hands in that dramatic way she had. "You mean it? About the room? You really mean it? Lester says so, too. No one else has seen this place except you two, so I just didn't know. I know *I* love it, but . . . ."

Claire broke in. "No, I didn't mean it. It's a rotten place." She saw what happened to Tillie-Rose's face at that. She didn't know how to take that kind of fooling around. I could have told her that Tillie-Rose always took everything at face value. You had to be careful with her. Claire said, "Aw, I was kidding. Silly-Tillie, it's a wonderful room. Really."

Then I said, "Tillie-Rose says I can take Alfie out of the hospital right now and he can stay here until I can get us fixed up. Once in a while I can visit, she says. Do you think it matters that it's dark and underground and he'd be alone a lot of the day?"

Tillie-Rose knew that wasn't exactly a fair presentation. "It wouldn't be like that really. You know I volunteer at the hospital and I know him. I know how to take care of him. He could help out upstairs and all. I just thought Lester would love the idea, and it'd be good

for Alfie, too. Why, he's practically an orphan, like me."
Tears at the brink for orphans.

Claire whirled to me. "Hey, I didn't know you were
still thinking of taking Alfie out! You didn't tell me." I
had really forgotten she didn't know.

She said to Tillie-Rose, "Uh-uh, forget it, this place
isn't for Alfie. It's a great place and all—for me, maybe,
not for him."

She stopped her nervous pacing and said to me, "But
that does give me an idea. If you're really going through
with this, then tell you what, Les. How about Alfie staying with me until you're set up. I mean, what do you
have in mind for you and Alfie?"

I told her about getting a real job and some money
together, and finding a little place of our own.

"Uh-huh. Well, then it will work out fine. I know it
will be all right with my folks. We have the room and I
know they've said lots of times how sorry they were for
him. So, what do you think?" She looked at me deeply.
"Remember this morning? Our talk in the lot? Well, I'm
thinking of quitting the clubs—baseball, track . . . kid
stuff, you know? I'm thinking I'll stay home more. I can
help take care of Alfie."

What was going on here? First Tillie-Rose and now
Claire! All of a sudden, I felt that things had gotten out
of hand. Alfie was *my* affair, *my* friend. I didn't care
what their reasons were; *I* was the one! Horning in like
this! I wanted help, not a takeover.

I didn't know how to answer Claire, so I didn't. I pulled
a Mrs. Brenner and jumped to something else. "Let's
first get Alfie out for a weekend. Let's worry about that

first. Mrs. Brenner says he has to be with a family, and I know my ma won't sign him out for me. I'll be lucky if he can just stay over once. So what do you think?"

Claire said she was sure her folks would help arrange a visit, and once I knew the weekend was going to happen, I fell immediately into a dream of us walking around together just like old times. Alfie, with his eyes on the ground, would look for matchcovers and tin foil while I talked and talked. I would tell him how it was with me, and he would listen and say, "Yeah, Les" or "Sure, Les," and we would be easy together, just like it used to be. I would tell him how I was going to save him from that hospital because it was no good for him. We had to stick together. We'd be okay together.

While I was dreaming, Tillie-Rose and Claire were getting on like a house afire. They were planning Alfie's weekend. Tillie-Rose asked what Alfie liked to do best. "We want to make sure he has the time of his life." I told her that he likes to walk around and collect things, that he likes to play with his stamps, that he likes to make money, to be busy, to work at anything. "He used to walk around and sell magazines," I told her. "I wish we could think up something for him to sell. He'd love that."

Claire stopped pacing around the room and clapped her hands together. "Sometimes I'm such a genius!" she said, pretending to swoon. "We can kill two birds with one stone. All we have to do is think of some way Alfie can take in money. He'd have a good time with that. And you just said you want to get some money ahead, so we can put that money away for when he comes out of the hospital for good. Like a fund, an Alfred Fund. Know what I mean?"

I didn't. But Tillie-Rose seemed to. She got all excited. "You mean, like have a fair or a show or something? Charge an entrance fee for kids? Alfie can collect the money? Like that? Hey! That's terrific. I can make all the decorations and yeah . . . we can have a real old-fashioned fair with games and stuff. Where? When?"

"No, no, not like that, I don't mean that exactly. First of all, kids aren't where the money is. We wouldn't make enough doing that. I really don't know what I mean yet. But it'll come." She was suddenly restless again. She shivered. Jamming her hands in her pockets, she went to the door. "C'mon, let's get out of here. I want to see the old neighborhood some more and I gotta get home soon."

We poked around a few of the old places and then we went to the beach. The private beach wasn't opened yet, not until June. All those handball courts and hand tennis courts stood empty, waiting for the summer people. The gate was closed tight, so we went to the free beach.

We walked along the shoreline where the sand was hard packed, and it was easier walking. That close to the water, the breeze was cutting. The gulls were swooping. Their lonesome cry suited me.

Claire leaned across me to ask Tillie-Rose, "How old are you, any way?"

"Almost fourteen. In June, fourteen."

"You have boyfriends?"

"Oh, sure. Well, no one who's especially mine, if that's what you mean. I'm sort of in love with Selwyn Sarkin.

Isn't that a beautiful name? Selwyn Sarkin. Only he doesn't know it. And there's Lester. You're my boyfriend, aren't you, Les? Only he's taken already." This with rolling eyes and a dig in my ribs. Claire didn't notice at all. Tillie-Rose didn't know how untaken I was.

"Well, I mean, you like boys and want to get married and all?" I shook my head, listening to that. My poor Claire, she didn't even know what she wanted to ask. What did she think she was going to get from Tillie-Rose?

Just then, a purple man ran out of the sea right in front of us. He was one of those crazies who go for a swim every day no matter what the weather. I think they would chop through ice to get in. They call themselves Polar Bears, and the purple man looked like one, he was so full of shaggy gray hair, from top to toe. He pranced on the beach, beating his body to warm up, flinging freezing drops our way. We shrank away and he laughed.

"A little water won't hoit. A swim every day keeps the doctor away! Do you good. Soft like sponge cake, you kids!" He saw me and his mistake at the same time. "Not you, young fella. For you, carrot juice! Every day, carrot juice. Fix you up and make you healthy, hear what I'm telling you?" He slapped his chest. "How old do you think I am?" he asked us coyly. He was at least sixty and wanted us to believe half that.

"Eighty-three," said Claire.

His face fell a mile. He turned away from us disgustedly, and we three fell into a severe case of the giggles. It made everything better.

When we recovered, we returned to Alfie. We agreed

89

that Tillie-Rose and I would stop off at Claire's on our way to the hospital tomorrow morning. Claire wanted us to ask Lena and Alex for their ideas about what to do with Alfie on the weekend. We hadn't even decided when it would be yet. Maybe they would think of something absolutely terrific.

Things were rolling along.

CHAPTER TWELVE

As it turned out, Lena did have a terrific idea. At least, she thought it was.

We were all sitting around her table upstairs, drinking tea and eating cookies. Tillie-Rose's eyeballs were practically falling out of her head looking around that wonderful kitchen and drinking tea with someone who looked and talked like a movie star.

Alex wasn't there at first. There was just Lena to tell about taking Alfie home for a weekend visit and that we wanted to give him a real good time. When Lena heard that, she shot me one of her dazzling smiles and said, "Ah, but yes. That's what I said, remember? That's very nice, a very good thing. Yes, just for a visit. Go on."

Claire told her we were trying to think of some way to give Alfie something to do, something he would really like, and at the same time raise money for an Alfred Fund. Money that could be put away for when Alfie would be staying with me for good.

Again, Lena glanced at me, and this time there was no smile. "So? You don't give up, do you?" She nodded her head as if she understood something.

Just then Alex walked in. He bent over Tillie-Rose's hand as they were introduced. I knew she wanted to faint dead away. It wasn't just his good looks, though I'm sure that counted plenty, but something foreign in his ways. He spoke as American as anyone, but it was like he stepped out of the pages of a book. Same with his mother, of course. But who wants to read all day?

Claire explained what we had just told Lena. He got it right away and right away came up with what I thought was a great idea. He said we ought to have a street fair, a block party. That was sort of the latest craze around Brooklyn. He pointed out that Alfie could sell cookies or whatever, and drinks, too, if he could handle that. That would take care of his being part of something. And the rest of us could organize the block . . . have an auction, sell old clothes and stuff, arrange folk dancing. The way he described it, it sounded just great to me.

I didn't have a chance to find out how the others felt. Lena squelched that, right away. I don't know how it was done, except there was just no resisting her. She said it was silly, we couldn't collect enough money, it was too hard to arrange. Before she was done, I found myself agreeing like an idiot.

Finally, she took her son's hand and stroked it. "Alex, my darling, I know what we will do. For that poor, unfortunate friend we shall give a concert. You and me. Hmmmm? We will play the music we have practiced together. That's the thing to do. We shall invite friends and neighbors and charge admission. . . ." Here she interrupted herself, stopped gazing into her son's eyes to look at us and to sweep the rest of us along. "Admission I said? Of course! That's where poor, dear Alfie can help —the way you so rightly wish for him. Is that not so? He can help collect the money."

Once I saw a snake charmer in Coney Island draw a snake out of a basket by just playing on some old horn. The snake seemed hypnotized by what he heard, weaving his head back and forth as the man played, slave to master. Same thing in the kitchen. Just like that snake, Tillie-Rose and Claire were practically glassy-eyed listening to Lena. Me too.

Lena turned to Alex again. "So, it's the thing to do, my darling boy; charge an admission so we indeed make money. It's not Carnegie Hall, but it will be a real concert. Someday, Carnegie Hall; but now, this. Everyone will hear what a splendid violinist my son is. And I am not so bad, either."

She stretched and wiggled her fingers, and all I can say is that it seemed absolutely settled that we would have this concert. At first, it seemed foolish when none of us—I mean none of the three of us—knew anything at all about that kind of music. It seemed like the last thing in the world for us to do. But as Lena talked, it began to sound real good. Like professional. I felt as if I should sit up straight and look wise, like a man who is deep into the higher things of life. Or maybe high on the deeper things of life.

Alex wouldn't do it.

"That's ridiculous, Lena!" he said. "My idea is better. I'm not ready for a concert; you know that. My nail hasn't healed yet. I think my violin should be looked at.

I'm not satisfied with the way it sounds lately. No, quite out of the question." He was pale as could be. He didn't mention he might be attacked by a bad case of dandruff, or that the earth might stop spinning by concert time. The thing was, he was scared to death of the idea, and I, for one, didn't blame him.

I waited for fireworks from Lena. Instead, just as calm as could be, she said, "Don't be silly, Alex, of course you will do it." She said this with such certainty that I knew there and then Alex was going to play us a concert. She sure had the power, that little woman.

"You want to be a violinist? You must begin. You are ready, my darling; there is only to start. How I would have leaped to this chance when I was your age! We will choose the program this very afternoon."

That question settled, she turned to us with her arms opened wide. "My dears, it will be a tremendous success, and we will make a lot of money for your friend! There is now only to decide when it will be. Two weeks from now? I think a Saturday night will be best, don't you? You can arrange for his weekend then? Very well, it's settled. I have many friends to invite: dancers, artists, musicians! Oh, my lovely Claire, your good heart has given us an opportunity!"

She embraced Claire, who sat still as a post. She didn't hug her back as she would ordinarily. I could see she even shrank into herself. Now what? Was she going to be afraid of simple affection all the rest of her life?

We began planning the evening: how much we should charge, how many people the house would hold, where we could borrow chairs—things like that.

We even decided to advertise. Tillie-Rose got all caught up in the idea of making posters and putting them in store windows.

All the while, Alex had something grumpy to say about everything we planned. Nothing pleased him—especially when it was something Lena suggested. I suddenly thought of the boy on the bus with his mother. Alex wasn't drumming his feet or humming, but it was the same sort of thing.

Well, Lena won hands down, and as I realized that, I knew that I wasn't jealous of him any longer. He was talented and handsome and healthy, but he had it tough, too. Like Claire. A sad idea came to me. Maybe they could help one another.

I watched Claire talking with Lena and Tillie-Rose, her face all lit up.

"Hey, why are you looking at me like that? Never mind, I don't want to know." She was all flash and tease again and it was a relief to me to let go of my thoughts.

Claire said, "Let's go to the hospital now. We're pretty much settled here. Okay?" She was up and at the door before I could stand.

As I pushed myself up from the chair, I said, "Tillie-Rose and I will take care of the posters, getting them into the stores and all, okay? What else has to be done?"

"Oh, much to do!" Lena said. "Claire, you will help Alex with the arrangements here, my darling?"

"Sure. Alex can help *me* with the arrangements, you mean. How about that, Alex?" said Claire.

He just nodded and looked so moody that I would have felt sorry for him, but I was really too tickled over this plan for Alfie and how it was all working out to worry about him.

Tillie-Rose had to check in when we got to the hospital, so we all parted ways. Claire went up to see Alfie and I went to see Mrs. Brenner.

As I walked the path to the administration building, I had to be careful not to bump into all the heavy traffic. Just one week made such a difference. This week it was spring, and the sun was out and so were all the patients, pushed in their wheelchairs by their visiting families. Some of the people I saw week after week, and we said hello to one another. The grounds were so neat and kept so pretty that I thought again what a shame it was such a nice place was so rotten for Alfie.

Right in front of Mrs. Brenner's building was the spastic guy I wanted to avoid. There was no avoiding him. "Buy a raffle? Buy a newspaper?" He spoke with such a contorted face I could hardly understand him. It always surprised me that he could sell raffles and newspapers. How could he keep track and make change and all? Poor guy. He gave me the willies, and I didn't know why. And I knew I was the last person in the world who should feel like that.

Mrs. Brenner was so pleased about the weekend visit you'd think I had given her a present. I told her Claire's parents would come get him, and she said she was sure Mr. Burt would be pleased, and she would tell them at the time about Alfie's medicines and things. "Ah, how nice for Alfie to have a change like this. That's the way, Lester. I'm glad to see you've given up the idea of taking him out for good."

96

I hated to see that smile of hers disappear.

"You're still planning to leave school—for him? Look for a job? Attach yourself to him?"

I felt like saying, "I do," like at a wedding. The sun was shining, and she looked so sad I wanted to see her smile again. She didn't. She sat at her desk, her feet not even touching the floor, like some aged doll, and in the most gentle voice in the world, said, "He'll not be getting any better, you realize that? He needs to be watched over, cared for, looked after. He's defective in mind and body and his seizures are not entirely under control. You realize all that and still want to take responsibility for him?"

We had been over this before. I knew she was making him so much worse than he really was just to scare me. I shut my ears to what she was saying and just nodded.

"And you still prefer to look after him rather than tend to your own life?"

She was pressing me.

"I'll be tending to my own life—with him! I'll have a better one—with him! We're a team. What's waiting for me, anyway? Pro football?"

"Without struggle and training, nothing much; that you can be sure of."

Her feet slapped the floor as she stood up. She walked me to the door. "You're off the track, Lester. I wish there was something that would turn you from this course you are on. Something that I could say or do that would show you."

She pointed to the window across the room. "Just look around outside."

Now what did she mean by that? Outside were only sick people.

Upstairs in Alfie's ward, Claire was straightening up his clothes that were squeezed into the small metal cabinet beside his bed. She showed me old bread, old pieces of sticky cake and other junk that she found hidden in the corners of the cabinet or in between his clothes.

I didn't know why he did that. "Maybe they don't feed him enough here," I said. I liked that idea, except I knew it wasn't true.

Claire told me Tillie-Rose had gotten a wheelchair for Alfie and told us to meet them downstairs. The idea of putting him in a wheelchair made me furious. He could walk!

I looked around the room. I said hello to Mrs. Benedict, who was spooning something into her husband's mouth. I never once saw him with his eyes opened, and every time I went there, his wife was feeding him something out of a jar that she brought from home. It's one of those things I couldn't stand thinking about. An old woman like that feeding all that was left of her husband —a mouth. The rest of the men were sleeping the day away.

We found Tillie-Rose and Alfie waiting for the elevator.

"Hey, Alfie, hi!" I sure was glad to see him. "You know you're coming home with me soon for a visit. What do you think of that!"

He wrinkled his forehead and looked worried. "Yeah,

she told me. What's her name again?" He meant Tillie-Rose and talked as if she wasn't there. It was so like him I laughed.

"You're looking good. What are you doing in the wheelchair?" It made him look smaller—and younger. He needed a haircut and his hospital clothes didn't fit. He couldn't close the top button of his pants.

"I don't wanna sit here," he said and began struggling to get out. "She told me to." Again he meant Tillie-Rose.

She said, "The floor nurse said I could take him out only in a wheelchair." She was all upset. "She said he falls a lot."

"See what I mean?" I said to both of them. "They're making him that way. He never needed a wheelchair before, did he, Claire? He walked fine."

Claire looked worried too. "But that was then. I don't know, Alfie, you okay? Can you walk?"

"Sure, sure I can." There was no keeping him. He was out and up.

We left the wheelchair outside the elevator and went outside to find a bench so we could talk. I was eager to tell Alfie about the concert and about his collecting the money at the door.

It was slow going because everyone had a good word for Alfie. He must have stopped at a hundred wheelchairs to say hello, and laugh just like a little kid when he was teased about who he was with.

"You're with your girl friends today, hey, Alfred?"

I never saw anybody so liked.

Then, because this was his home and he could show us around, he plunged ahead, leaning forward as if battling a wind. Suddenly, he toppled over, almost hitting the side of a bench.

Alfie paid no attention to his fall at all, but the rest of us were shook up. You never knew with Alfie if he's hurt himself or not because he never complains. I never heard him say he was hurt, and I remembered hearing something once about him having this peculiar thing of not feeling pain.

We all sat, and Alfie shook my shoulder and like old times grinned at me. "Hey, Les, I wanna tell you something." He lowered his voice as if he had a secret to tell me. "Hey, Les, I think I'm gettin' out of polio." He held his bad hand up for me to see. I knew that his mother told him he had had polio, because it was an easy word for him to remember. Actually, he was left the way he was after having a very high fever and convulsions when he was a baby. Not polio at all. "Looka here. See that?" His hand looked the same to me. Smaller than the other, the whole arm short, it was trembling with the effort to hold it up.

"I don't see anything different, Al. What do you mean?"

"See, I can hold it up? And my leg feels different at night when I go to sleep. So what I think is that I'm gettin' out of polio!"

Claire and I exchanged a look in which there was something of alarm. Alfie never had weird ideas before.

Claire got us all some ice cream from the canteen, and Alfie gave it his whole attention. Then, when he was finished, he sat the cup on the bench next to him and went away from us. I mean, he was there, but he just sat, rubbing his hand, not paying the least mind to us any-more. He never used to do that. He was always so alert, following everything with curious eyes. It was a little gift from the hospital, and I was seeing it more and more.

I told him about the concert and how he would help collect money at the door. Even that didn't rouse him.

"Yeah, sure," he said, as if it were old news to him. Then something occurred to him. "You mean I'm leaving the hospital?"

Again we told him the good news: for a weekend, soon. More later. Yes.

And what did he say to that? "I don't know if my mother would like that."

This really floored me. "Alfie, you know, you know your mother is dead." I was scared to death that somehow he had forgotten or didn't believe it.

"Yeah, she passed away two years ago." A flat statement. "My father put me here so he could work," he said, rubbing his hand, his eyes absent again.

All the way home, I was as depressed as could be. It was Tillie-Rose who gave me something hopeful to hang on to.

She said, "When you get him home with you, he'll be different. You'll see. He'll be his old self again."

CHAPTER THIRTEEN

Somehow the days passed without me being in them. What I mean is that nothing seemed real to me except the future—the weekend with Alfie, the concert, and then the time after that when the two of us would be together and my real life would begin. So, I just went through the motions and eating and school and yes, Ma and no, Ma. When I thought of Claire, it was only to push it away again—too much for me to grapple with now. It was like the idea of staying up late when I was a kid—a treat for the future. It was only with Tillie-Rose that I felt all there. There was something about her . . . simple, like good bread. When I was with her, I felt my creases all smoothed out.

Every day after school I went to the butcher shop and we made the deliveries together. And every chance I had, I went down to her wonderful room just to think or do my homework or make up stories in my head about the future. The escape hatch, I called it.

Tillie-Rose had made a terrific poster to put in store windows. She had drawn a funny picture of a violin with wings and a halo, fluttering in the sky like a butterfly. Hanging from it was a banner that said: HELP THIS VIOLIN DO A GOOD DEED. COME TO A CONCERT. Then at the bottom she lettered:

Date: Sat. April 7, 1939, 8 P.M.
Players: Alex and Lena Lensky
1865 E. 12th St.
Admission: .75¢

FOR THE ALFRED FUND   FOR THE ALFRED FUND

It was a beaut.

She made about a dozen copies, and then about a week before the concert, we took the train to Claire's neighborhood and put them in the store windows. I thought the store owners would be glad to let us do it, that it would give a store a little class, advertising a fancy concert and all. You'd think we were giving away rabies.

We finally placed them all, but I was exhausted by the time we got home, and my day hadn't ended yet. I had a talk with my mother to look forward to. I had good news and bad news. I was going to invite her to the concert and then ask her about Alfie staying with us Saturday night. I couldn't bear not having him in the bed next to me that night. After the concert, we could all go home together. I have a mind like a fairy tale because I could already see us sitting around the kitchen drinking Ma's cocoa, Ma fussed and friendly, urging cookies on us, just a cozy group.

After supper, when she was putting laundry away in my dresser drawer, was the moment, I felt. She was humming a tune I had heard all my life. It was from her own childhood in the old country and it meant she was in a good mood.

Pa was out of the question. Saturday was his poker night, and nothing short of a fatal accident would stop him from going. So there was just my mother.

"Ma, how would you like to come to a concert with me Saturday night?"

She straightened up and beamed at me. She had heard the words "come" and "with me" and didn't need any others. She sat on the bed next to me and smoothed my hair. "A what?"

"A concert, Ma. Somebody I know, a friend of mine, is going to play the violin and his mother is going to play the piano. It's like a duet."

"So. That's nice. They want company for that?"

"Not exactly company, Ma. It's more like an audience, like a play you go to. You pay admission. But I'm taking you. You're my guest." I raised her hand to my lips because I realized it was the first time I had taken *her* someplace. I was filled with love for her.

"That's very nice, Lester. And where will this be, this concert?"

She was suddenly a bit formal, and I think it was because I used the word "guest." I knew her well enough to see she was a bit shy with that.

That made me feel closer to her than I had felt for ages. It didn't seem fair that she didn't know what I had in mind for me and Alfie. It wasn't fair, and besides, she had to know sometime. So . . . I told her.

I had expected—I don't know what. At that particular

moment, maybe, it was understanding and love pats. If I were thinking right, it would be anger or a shouting match. What I didn't expect was such deep . . . mourning. She was so quiet and bowed you'd think a stone sat on her shoulders.

"Aw. Come on, Ma, I'm not dead or anything. I'm starting a new life is all. A better one. You'll see, it'll be great!"

She raised her eyes to me and I had to turn away from the look in them. "You're going to stop your chances, leave school, let yourself be . . . a, a nothing, a piece of garbage? All for this boy who is so bad in the head and bad in the body he has to be in a hospital yet? I don't understand you at all. What's going on with you, Lester? What's going on in your head? How can you do this to yourself?"

What's the use of trying to explain something to someone who thinks the world is just waiting for me with open arms?

When I didn't say anything, she smoothed her apron, gave it a final pat and stood up. "All right, my son. I'll go to the concert. Also, Alfred can stay here Saturday night in that bed."

She nodded at the twin across the room. "After that, no. He goes back to the hospital Sunday?"

I nodded yes.

"When you decide he's to come out of that place for good, then you make other plans. He stays someplace else, but not here. You're going to get a place of your own? Move out of your mother's house? On what, I'd like to know?" I had never heard her so bitter. "Well,

I'm not a party to your plans any more. You think you're a grown person who doesn't need his mother, so you have to figure."

She looked around the room as if it would tell her what she should say next. Her voice was shaking.

"All right, never mind you, never mind what you do to yourself. Think about him, your friend Alfred. If anything happens to that boy, it's on your head, you understand? Yours. Not mine or any one else's."

That was her parting shot. When in doubt, use guilt as a weapon.

"That's okay, Ma. Nothing's going to happen."

CHAPTER FOURTEEN

The day of the concert I was up and over to Claire's before the Ellingers had finished breakfast. We were all going in the car to fetch Alfie, and I was as excited and nervous as a little kid.

"Sit down, Lester. We'll be through in a minute." That was Claire's mother sounding like the teacher she is. "Claire, finish your egg, that's a dear."

"Don't want any." She pushed her chair back impatiently. "Come on, finish up and let's go, everybody. Dad, can I borrow your sweater for Alfie? I think it's windy out, and I don't know if he has one. Does he, Les?"

Does he? I had a brief flash of panic. I hadn't thought of clothes at all. So much to think of! Claire saw my confusion.

"He could be naked for all you know!" That really stung. It wasn't her business anyway.

"Calm down, Claire," said her father, pointing his cereal spoon at her. "Go in the next room if you're finished, and we'll be along soon. You're as jumpy as a cat."

"I'm sorry, Les. Dad's right, I am jumpy. Here, you can kick me." Her behind, which gave her so much trouble and me such pleasure, was turned to me as we entered her room. I noticed right away there was a record player on top of her desk and a stack of records next to it.

"Hey, what's all this?"

She immediately clasped one of the albums to her chest as if I were going to snatch it from her. I could see it had a picture of a whole orchestra on it. Claire said, "This all belongs to Alex; he lent it to me. Listen, Les, something amazing happened to me the other night."

"Uh-oh," I said, rolling my eyes.

She laughed. "No, not that, you dummy. I'm talking about music. I've been trying to learn about music—classical music, like the Lenskys play, you know?"

No, I didn't know.

"So, I've been listening upstairs once in a while, and it was nice and all, but the other night I had a real experience." She said that as if it had capitals on it. "Alex put on this record, see, and the violins were swirling and swirling around . . . ." Claire now was swirling around the room, telling me this with absolute wonder in her voice. "And all of a sudden, it was like a thunderclap. It was like I had cotton in my ears all my life and suddenly it dropped out and I could hear!"

She stopped moving around and declared for maybe the hundredth time since I've known her, "I'm in love!"

I couldn't help snorting.

"Go ahead, laugh, but I'm telling you, all I want to do is listen to this music. I can't get enough. Here, let me put this on and you listen!"

I stopped her. She wasn't the only jumpy one. All I was interested in was the concert upstairs.

"Some other time, really, Claire. I'll listen some other time. I just want to know: Everything ready upstairs?"

"Yep. We borrowed enough chairs yesterday to seat an army. I only hope someone comes. Can you smell what Lena is baking? She was at it all day yesterday, too, either practicing or baking. God, I wish it were over."

"How's Alex? I don't hear him practicing. Is he having his nervous breakdown yet? Hey! No hitting! I was only kidding."

Claire found something interesting to look at out the window. Her back was to me when she said, "Speaking of Alex, I want to tell you something." Her back didn't tell me whether it was good or bad. I got ready, as if I were going over a roller coaster.

"You know, we've been together a lot recently, me and Alex, getting ready for the concert and talking, listening to music, just hanging out together more than we used to. Well, I thought . . . ." She mumbled something to the windowpane.

"What? For heaven's sake, Claire, come and sit down. I can't hear you."

She came behind me and began shouting in my ear like I was deaf. "Can you hear me now?" She rolled up a newspaper and held it to my ear like a funnel. "Getting a little hard of hearing, are you?"

I tried to grab the newspaper from her, wanting only to get her talking again. I was afraid her folks would come in any minute and I was dying to hear.

"Cut it out, Claire. Stop fooling around and tell me."

She sat down then, hung on to one of my hands and got serious. "You know what I told you, Les? About myself and not knowing? Not knowing if what those people said about me was true or not, about me being queer and all? Well, I thought I would try it with Alex."

It? She thought she would try *it?* Had they already . . . ?

"So—I got him to kiss me." I could have laughed out loud. I had forgotten how green she was. "He likes me, but I know as sure as I'm sitting here that he only thought of me like a pal, you know, not like a girl friend. So a few nights ago, we came in from a walk and he was going back upstairs—and so I asked him to. I wanted to see how it felt—how *I* felt. And I thought to myself I would go further if I liked it. You know what I mean?"

I knew what she meant. I squeezed her hand and she looked at me full and giggled. "You should have seen the look on his face when I asked him. Like he ate something he thought was blah and it turned out to be a chocolate éclair."

"What happened?" I cried.

"What happened was that he was all over me in a flash. I mean, he must be just crazy about chocolate éclairs! We were standing in the kitchen, against the door that goes up to his place, and he just leaned on me and kissed me and his hands all of a sudden went everywhere. I mean he had a thousand of them and they were all over me at once. Lena calls them 'his golden hands,' and with that many, he must be worth a fortune. Here, I'll show you." Her hands started flying around and wound up tickling me. She was driving me crazy fooling around.

I got hold of her hands. "So?" I gasped.

"So—what I mean to tell you is that I didn't get to learn anything. I was so busy fending him off I couldn't concentrate on the kissing. And you know why I was pushing him away? Not because I didn't want it. But every minute that was going on, all I could think of was how disappointed those 'golden hands' must be when they didn't feel anything upstairs. You know?" She indicated where her boobs were supposed to be—but weren't. "It's really embarrassing!"

I didn't know whether to laugh or cry, torn between jealousy and amusement. "Oh, Claire," I moaned. It really hurt to hear all this. Yet . . . what a kid she was still.

"I know, I know," she waved an impatient hand at me. "You think it doesn't matter not having breasts, huh? Well, *you* try it for a change."

Then she said, "Oh, Lester, it's so good to be able to laugh over this with you. Why can't I just forget all this sex business, and you and me and Alfie live together!"

My mouth went dry with wanting. The three of us! But I wasn't ready to give up the "sex business." I was maybe greener than she was as far as actual experience went, but I was ready—man, was I ready! And she was running to me because I wasn't in the running.

She wasn't finished yet. "I don't want you to think I didn't sort of enjoy it, though—all that stuff with Alex. When I stopped him, he just dropped his hands and said okay, and then kissed me friendly like and went upstairs. So, we're still okay, and some time I might try it again. What do you think?"

111

She never found out what I thought because at that moment her mother and father called to us that they were ready to go.

There was no trouble at all. Claire's mother and father checked out with Mrs. Brenner. Alfie was ready and waiting and stepped into the car as if it were his. I had to roll up the window on his side so he wouldn't ride all the way with his head sticking out the window like a back-seat dog. I mean he really enjoyed that ride; one hand in mine, his eyes only on the passing streets. By noon, we were back at Claire's with Alfie in the car and the whole afternoon before us.

First we went upstairs to introduce him to Lena and Alex. Lena handed him a cookie right away and said she was very glad to meet him. "Same here," said Alfie and thanked her for the cookie. His mother was always careful about his manners, and I was proud he knew what to say.

Alex stopped practicing and came in to be introduced. I could see he was confused when Alfie stuck out his small bad hand, but Alex grasped it and pumped it. "Nice to meet you," he said, just as nice as if he were meeting a professor. I couldn't help watching his hands, knowing that they had been running over more than his violin strings. "Is Alfie going to help out at the door tonight?" he asked me.

Well, that was one of the big reasons we had planned the whole thing. I showed Alfie where we were going to stand at the door and the pocketbook Lena gave us to put the money in. He couldn't seem to get what the whole thing was about, but I knew he would understand better when he was actually doing it.

"It's going to be a real concert!" I said to Lena joyfully. I was beginning to see it all happen now that I had Alfie with me. I began to feel as if we were the cleverest people in the whole world to have arranged it all.

"Of course it's a real concert!" said Lena. "Now we must practice more, me and my son. You three must leave. I expect you back here at seven-thirty, and not before. We will have everything ready by then. Where will Alfie be having his dinner? Is he going home with you, Lester?"

I told her we decided it was easier for him to stay here at Claire's while I went home to change and get my ma. Easier for him and my ma, too. But after, after the concert, why then Alfie was going home with me to sleep overnight.

Lena said to Alfie, just to tease, "Don't stay up all night and smoke cigarettes and drink whiskey, Alfie. You have to promise me you won't do that."

This just about tickled him to death. "No, no I wouldn't smoke. I don't even drink any beer. No, no, don't worry." He kept shaking his head and laughing, too, trying to reassure her so she wouldn't stay up all night worrying about his bad habits, and at the same time loving the whole idea.

Claire shoved us out the door, knowing that I had my heart set on being just the two of us again for a while. Out on the street, I was ready to forget everything but just being together and alone, for once, and able to have all afternoon to do whatever we wanted.

The neighborhood was new to him, so I had to take him around. We walked around the streets and then to the train station and back. In about two seconds he had the whole layout in his head. He knew just where he was and where Claire's house was and everything. It was some funny kind of freak talent he was born with.

I could imagine what a funny pair we made, like Laurel and Hardy. I felt like a long pale rope compared to him. Especially since he'd gotten a little fat and maybe more bent over on one side.

I didn't care what we looked like. Just as I dreamed in my mind, I talked and talked to him as we walked along the streets. He was always such a . . . restful person for me to be with because he never expected anything of me, nothing more than what I could easily give. Before he was put away in that hospital, I was the one person necessary to him outside his house, just as his mother was, inside. Not to get anything from, but just to be there.

That was one happy afternoon for me. I talked and he listened and said "yeah" or "no" or "gee, Les," all the while keeping his eyes on the sidewalk, casing the trash cans, glancing in the cracks, in the gutters. The streets were his private bank. Other people thought a match-cover, a paper cigar ring, a Popsicle stick, was junk to throw away. But to Alfie, they were as good as money any day.

We stood on the corner of Coney Island Avenue, near the movie house, watching the trolleys go by. I brought up old times, when we used to walk around together every day. Alfie really perked up then. He had a

better memory than anybody for some things. I was re-
minding him of an old red wagon we used to pull around,
looking for wood, and asked him if he remembered.

"Yeah, sure I remember. I remember. It had a rusted
wheel. Hey, Les, whatever happened to that old wagon?"

"I don't know. Maybe it's still down there in the paint
room."

"Where we had cake? Remember that, hey, Les?"

Back and forth, back and forth, both of us remembering like two old men talking about the good old days. I
felt suddenly afraid, listening to us. I felt caught in
some no man's land between good old yesterday and
scary tomorrow, and right then would have given anything to go backward.

Alfie fell silent, and I asked him, "How about an egg
cream?" I had saved that as the biggest treat for him,
his favorite drink. We always used to save our money for
one. He'd always ask me why they call it an egg cream
when it only had syrup and milk and fizz in it, and I'd
always say I didn't know. Like a routine it was. So I had
a nickel with me for that, saving it as a surprise. I was
the surprised one. "No, thanks," said Alfie.

Well, then I had to look at him, see what was wrong.
His face looked . . . pinched. "You cold, Alfie?" I asked.
The wind was up and papers were swirling around, dust
stinging my eyes once in a while. He was wearing Claire's
father's sweater, which was about two sizes too big and
turned up around the wrists so his hands were free. I
knew he never noticed the cold before, but maybe the
hospital had made him different that way.

"Naw, naw," he said, but didn't smile. I didn't like the

way he looked. I tried to put it out of my mind as we walked on.

I guess an hour must have passed. We were standing looking in the window of Ebinger's bakery. I pointed to my favorite chocolate cake, called Othello, and said how we were going to share a whole one some day, just the two of us. Suddenly, Alfie said, "I want to go home now." He looked more bent over than ever. The whites of his eyes were yellowish, like boiled onions, and his color was funny.

"Sure," I said. It was time, anyway, getting on to four-thirty. "You feeling all right?" I asked him. In my heart, I felt a knot of worry. I knew it really didn't mean anything when he said he was.

On the way home, I told him how we were going into business someday. He needn't think he was going to stay in the hospital all his life. No siree. He was going to come and live with me just as soon as I could swing it. I told him all the things I had been stewing over and just let them sink into him, like tossing troubles down a well. I told him about Claire and how there would never be anyone else for me—how could there be?—but with us together, who needed women? I told him how popular he was all of a sudden, Claire and Tillie-Rose both wanting him, both having their reasons, of course. I told him all the things I told no one else. Alfie just limped slowly beside me, not saying a word. He was taking it all in without a bit of surprise, just the way he greeted everything.

We got back to Claire's house, and I told him I would see him later. He just stood there, picking on his sweater, while I said good-by. I wasn't sure he was listening to me. Even his lips were gray. What could be wrong with him? It occurred to me that it was a big change for him to be out of the hospital. Sure. And he probably was excited and worried about the evening. That was why he didn't look so hot.

"Hey, don't worry," I told him. "It'll be fine tonight. Nothing to it. Just a bunch of people to take money from, okay? Claire?" She came in from the kitchen. "We're back. I gotta go now."

Claire helped Alfie off with his sweater. "Go ahead, Les. See you later," she said. To Alfie she growled, "You're all mine now."

"'By, Alfie," I said. I didn't hear his answer because his face was hidden in the yellow woolen folds.

I was going to tell her that I didn't think Alfie looked so good, but then I thought, what for? He'll settle down. He'll have a great time tonight. It's his night.

CHAPTER FIFTEEN

It was his night all right.

I don't think I'll ever forget where I was and what I was doing when that phone call came. It's like a snapshot in my mind. I see my ma at the sink, her hands in sudsy water washing the dishes. An apron covers her good black dress with the shiny beads all over the front. Her head was turned to me, her cheeks pink with the steam from the hot water. She was speaking, her lips parted wide enough for me to see her gold tooth. I had a dishtowel in one hand and was drying a bowl. I was dressed and ready to go, too. The jacket of my good blue suit was hanging over the top of a kitchen chair. My shirt sleeves were rolled up and I, too, had on a long apron so I wouldn't drop food on my good pants. My head was raised. I was smiling at my mother. The telephone rang. And that's how I will always see us when I think of that night.

The phone rang and I answered. It was Claire.

As soon as I heard her voice, I knew something bad had happened. She said, "I can't talk now. They're getting in the car with Alfie. He has to get back to the hospital, Lester. He's sick! One hundred and two on the thermometer! He looks awful and we don't know what's wrong. Les? You there, Lester?"

I managed to grunt.

"So my folks are taking him back to the hospital. He *has* to go back. My folks are frantic, you can imagine. I have to stay here. For upstairs. The concert. What do you think can be the matter with him? Oh, God, isn't this awful! Please, Les, come over right away!"

While I was listening to this, Tillie-Rose had come in, and I guess what I was hearing was written all over my face. She and Ma kept asking, "What's the matter? What's the matter?" I had to wave to them to be still.

I fought for control so I could talk, but what was there to say? "We'll be right there, Claire."

I told Ma and Tillie-Rose, and in the telling, I realized what I should have told Claire.

"I'm not going. You two go. I'm going to the hospital."

Everything that night seems to stand out so clearly. Tillie-Rose looked good. For the first time, I saw her dressed up in a skirt and blouse instead of her old bulky sweat shirt. Her hair was pulled back in a ponytail with a red bow, and no question, she looked good. Mainly it was her face, glowing like a flower with glasses. She clasped her hands and cried.

"This is the worst thing that ever happened! Oh, Lester, I'm coming with you!"

She was going to go on with it, but I wasn't about to listen. "Please, Tillie-Rose, take my ma to Claire's and help out at the concert. We can't both leave it just like that. You have to take our place at the door. Go on, please."

It was minutes of such confusion. It's a wonder we didn't put Ma on the bus to Alfie's and me on a train to the Bronx. Somehow, we sorted it out. We walked together to the station because I could get my bus there. I promised I would call and let them know what's what as soon as I could.

"Tell Lena I'm sorry, awfully sorry. And I hope the concert comes off okay. Don't worry about me."

Why shouldn't they worry about me? I was a wreck by the time I got to the hospital. At that time of night, the buses don't run too often. I could have bitten my nails down to my wrists I was so anxious to get there.

I teetered past the gate and hadn't the least idea where to go. I decided to check his ward first.

I was almost to the elevator when I was stopped by a nurse. "Visiting hours are over," she said. "You can't go up now."

I explained about taking out one of the patients that morning, and he was taken sick and brought back to the hospital.

"I've got to see him, find out how he is."

She asked me his name and told me to wait and she would call his floor to find out if he was there.

I passed the time by trying to identify the sounds I heard. It was weird being in the hospital at night. I'd never been there before so late. It felt so dim and hushed, as if I should even think in whispers. No one was around, not a soul, not a wheelchair in sight. All the patients were upstairs in their rooms I supposed. Somewhere close, I could hear the slaps and bangings of the kitchen workers, and I could hear the creaking of the elevator. I hated every minute of it.

The nurse came back. "He's upstairs. The doctors are with him. Are you a relative? They said only relatives are allowed to go up."

"Yes, I am," I lied.

Green curtains were drawn around Alfie's bed, and that scared me. I could see lots of feet under it. Then the curtain opened, and one of the doctors came out and hurried away. The curtain was open long enough for me to see Alfie, and long enough for him to see me. He was lying on the bed, wearing a hospital gown, and two more doctors were talking to one another over his head. Alfie looked at me and I swear I never saw such a look on anyone's face before. His eyes! His eyes looked wild with fear, like some dumb, terrified animal. Really not a human look, but an animal look.

I managed to say, "Hiya, Alfie," just to let him know someone was there who knew him and cared about him. The curtain closed again.

I stood staring at it, and a nurse came by and touched my arm and was kind to me. She told me softly to go to the lounge where the people with Alfie were waiting. She told me that the doctors were going to take Alfie to another building for an operation. I just couldn't open my mouth to ask why.

Claire's parents were surprised to see me. They each took one of my hands and sat me between them on the leather couch. Mrs. Ellinger said, "He wouldn't eat, and when I touched his forehead, it was burning up. He looked so bad I knew he must be sick. Isn't that right, Sam? Didn't we know he was sick even before we sat down? I remember his mother. Such a nice woman."

Mr. Ellinger picked up the story. "We asked if he felt sick, and he said no. We asked him if anything hurt, and he said no. And when we took his temperature, it was way up. So, Lester, we had to bring him back here. We are responsible for him. I have no idea what's wrong, and apparently, the doctors don't know yet, either. They told us there was no point in staying, but we are hoping to hear some news."

Then a nurse came in to the lounge and said, "You the people waiting for Burt? Alfred Burt? He's being taken to the operating room now. That's the next building over. You can stay in the waiting room there, but it might be hours, you know. Call in the morning, why don't you?"

Mr. Ellinger stood up and said firmly, "That's that. I think we should be going. Come on, Irene. Lester?"

I couldn't go and I couldn't stay. I was stuck.

Mrs. Ellinger said, "Don't look like that, Lester, he'll be all right. He's in good hands."

More heartily, her husband said, "He sure is. I should have it so good. He has more doctors looking after him than I ever will. He'll be all right. Now, you can't stay here. The busses stop running soon, you know."

They took me home. Not to their place; it was too late for that. The concert was over by then. As they stopped in front of my house, I suddenly realized what a rotten evening these people had had instead of listening to nice music. I didn't know how to say it.

"I'm sorry. Thanks for the ride, and . . . thanks for Alfie . . . and I'm sorry." Like a little kid.

Ma was home already and waiting up.

"So, how is he?"

"I don't know, Ma. They don't know. They are going to operate on him, so it must be serious. How was the concert?"

"A beautiful player he is, that Alex, and his mother, too. It's too bad you missed it. A lot of people. Where are you going?"

"To bed, Ma."

"First, you should call Tillie-Rose. She said no matter what time, you should call. She's a nice girl."

She followed me to the telephone. "I didn't mean it, Lester, about it being on your head if anything happened to Alfie. I didn't mean it, and now I could bite out my tongue." I wouldn't listen. I couldn't listen.

I told Tillie-Rose what I knew, and she said she would go with me to the hospital the next morning whenever I wanted. We didn't talk long because I was longing for my own bedroom and to stop this talking and to be alone. I told her I was glad the concert was fine and that I'd hear about it in the morning. I had to listen to her tell me not to worry, just like Claire's folks. Not to worry, not to worry. Christ, if I couldn't worry over this, what should I worry about? Finally I was back in my room and able to just look into the darkness from my bed.

After a few hours of that, I crept to the kitchen to call the hospital.

I was told his appendix had burst. I was told they couldn't save him. I was told he was dead. So sorry.

CHAPTER SIXTEEN

After that, I didn't know what to do with myself. I couldn't find any place to put my body, so I got dressed and went out. It wasn't even dawn yet, just a faint light in the sky to show morning was coming. Not a soul was up at that hour, so I had the streets to myself, like in my dream. Not even those magic sneakers would help me now; I couldn't bound my way out of this one. The wind was cutting, but I headed for the beach anyhow, out of habit almost. In my bad moments, the sight of the ocean seems to help. I could smell the faint seaweed air as I walked along, and suddenly that wasn't the place I wanted to be. I didn't want to be soothed by the sight of the ocean, or hear the gulls cry, or like where I was. I didn't want to be out in the world at all. If there was a hole to crawl into, some place dark where I could hide and not come out ever, I would head for that—Tillie-Rose's room!

The basement door was unlocked, as usual, and I lit the candle that was kept on the ledge. I headed for that room, positively thirsting for it, the closed door, the mattress on the floor and the complete dark.

I sank down on the bed, blew out my candle and gave myself up to what was waiting for me. It wasn't tears and it wasn't grief. What I had to face was my anger. It bowled me over. Not anger at the fates or anger at the cruuuel, cruuuel world that took away my friend. It was anger at my dead friend himself, Alfie the Innocent, who went and left me. I shook with this knowledge of myself, overwhelmed by the ugliness I found there. So this is what I was like: Alfie dies and I'm mad at him.

Swept by anger, and something else—panic—I groaned aloud and twisted on the bed, knocking over the orange crate and candles. The crash on the floor nearly stopped my heart.

A door slammed upstairs, and then footsteps. Someone was coming in the basement door. If I could have wrung my hands just then, I would have. The last thing in the world I wanted was to talk to another person at that moment.

Tillie-Rose's scared voice said, "Who's there? Come on out. I have a . . . a . . . a gun here, and I'll shoot, you betcha. Who is it?"

"Don't shoot me, Tillie-Rose." Another time I would have laughed.

She pushed open the door, holding the flashlight she was going to shoot me with.

"You! Lester!" I waved away the bright light that was blinding me. She lit some candles. She knelt on the floor beside the bed and searched my face.

"Alfie?" she whispered. I didn't answer.

"Dead?" she whispered.

I had no warning at all. I didn't expect what happened then at all. From nowhere, from everywhere, there rose in me this . . . storm. I couldn't believe those sounds came from me. The tears just leaped from my eyes. I wet the whole front of her bathrobe. Just those two words from her did it. Unlocked me. The amazing thing was that I wasn't feeling anything at all. It was more like one of Alfie's seizures than grief. Just amazing. But, my God, it helped.

Finally, I was able to push her arms away and lie down. I was completely done in.

"Thanks," I managed to say.

She stood over me. "Want to talk?" Ready to talk, ready to go, whatever I wanted.

I felt clear-sighted, as if the tears had washed the hogwash away. I didn't want to talk, but I grabbed at her bathrobe like a lifeline. "You don't know. It's not just Alfie—it's me. You don't know what I am."

She knelt. "Lester? Of course I know. Hey, it's no shame to cry over a friend. I know your heart is broken and all."

"No, no, it's not that! I'm no friend. I see that now. I'm a phony, that's what I am. I thought everybody was using Alfie but me. I thought I was the only pure one, the one true friend. Christ, what horseshit!"

"What are you talking about? You *are* a true friend. Everyone in the world knows that!"

She was making me frantic. "Listen, Tillie-Rose. You've got to understand. I was the biggest user of all. I just kidded myself that I was saving him. I thought . . . boohoo, poor Alfie, in the hospital and needs to be rescued. I thought I really cared about him, really had his good in mind, and all the time, what he was, was an excuse for me. That's all. Don't you see? I hid behind him because I couldn't face what it takes to make it as a cripple in this world. Did he have to die for me to see that? Now do you see?"

Emotion was strangling me, the words strung together, spilling from me in one long, ropy whine. No one in the world could have understood me just then, and Tillie-Rose couldn't and didn't want to. All the while she was holding and patting, her face was set against knowing what I was trying to say. From someplace she pulled a blanket. "I don't know what you're talking about. Only that Alfie's dead, and that's making you think things, say things that aren't so." She stood up and covered me. "You ought to sleep now, instead of saying bad things about yourself."

She blew out the candle and found the door with her flashlight. "I'll call your ma and tell her you're here. Go to sleep now."

What's the use? drifted across my mind, and then I was asleep.

Someone was shaking me, and I opened my eyes to see Claire. I felt as sore and tender inside as a baby. Just the sight of her made the tears rise, only this time they were weak tears like an invalid.

"Alfie's dead," I said. "His appendix burst. You know?"

"I know," said Claire, sitting beside me on the mattress. "I can't believe it, but I know." In the candlelight, she looked like a ghost. "Tillie-Rose called me and my folks called the hospital." She picked up my hand. "I can't believe it."

"Yeah."

"You think if we didn't take him out he would still be . . . ?"

"Don't, Claire," I said, sitting up. That was not a conversation I was about to have, not even to think about. I had enough to struggle with. That one was for later.

She pointed to the ceiling. "Tillie-Rose is making something to eat. Want something?"

I was suddenly famished.

Tillie-Rose put a plate before me, everything already cut up. Steak! One good thing about having a father who owns a butcher store. The three of us sat around the table being terribly polite to one another, as if we had all been in some kind of accident.

For a while, we just ate and didn't say a word. Then, almost in whispers, they began to tell me about the concert. They avoided Alfie, but all roads led to him. Tillie-Rose was telling me about a speech Lena made afterward, after all the applause. "Did you hear what some man shouted about Alex?" she asked Claire. " 'Another spaghetti!' he said out loud. Isn't that a funny thing to say about his playing?"

Claire looked disgusted. " 'Szigeti,' he said. Not spaghetti. Some great violinist, he meant." As if Tillie-Rose should know that.

"Oh, well then, so Lena was thanking them for coming and all and said how sorry she was they couldn't meet Alfie because it was thanks to him that every one got to hear her son's beautiful violin playing. It was thanks to the Alfred Fund. . . ."

Tillie-Rose broke off. The same thought struck us. The

Alfred Fund! It hit my stomach like a ton of bricks. I hadn't realized when I was counting up that even Lena and Alex had used Alfie in some way, for their own sakes. There was so much riding on him, so much more in that Alfred Fund than money. And now all we had was the money.

"Flowers?" murmured Claire. She was poking the food around on her plate and didn't look up. She didn't see me shake my head. Whatever we did with that money, that wasn't it.

Tillie-Rose broke the silence.

"Hey, did you hear the fight in the bedroom before Lena and Alex came out to play?" she asked Claire, who stoped playing with her food and raised her head at this.

"What fight?"

"Alex and Lena. It was loud as anything. I heard when I went to the bathroom. Alex was mad at her for getting him into this, he said, and said he was sick and wasn't going to do it. Wasn't going to play, *couldn't* play, he said. I thought I'd die—people already sitting in the chairs in the living room and he wasn't going to play. Well, you should have heard Lena lace into him. I don't blame her; it was too late for him to back out and all. But how they talked to one another! Their voices! It was like they hated one another. But, hey, I think now she shouldn't push him to play if he doesn't want to. You know? I don't mean last night. She shouldn't push him altogether. She's the one who wants it, not him. So it's more for her, right? What do you think?"

Tillie-Rose leaned forward on her elbows, her hands

cupping those big cheeks, and really wanted to hear what Claire had to say about this.

"You think he hates her or what?" she persisted.

Claire said, "Don't be dumb. What do you mean, 'hates her'? Of course he doesn't *hate* her!"

"Well, that's some funny kind of love then, on both sides."

"So? So it's a funny kind of love! So what? Maybe there are lots of funny kinds. Who made up rules about it, anyway?"

She shoved away her plate and glared at Tillie-Rose. A fight. That's all I needed.

"Okay, okay, I was only talking. Don't get sore." Tillie-Rose raised her hands as if surrendering to an army. She had no idea why it was such a touchy subject with Claire. She tried to pass it off as a joke.

"Hey, any kind's a good kind, I say. I'd take any old kind myself."

It was at me that Claire looked when she said, "You bet, Tillie-Rose. Any old kind is a good kind. What do you think, Les?"

I didn't have a thought in my head.

What I said was, "I don't know. I'm no expert on any thing. What I think is that I'm going to the hospital now. No, no." I could see they were about to get up, about to go with me. "No, I'd rather go alone. Really. Say, Tillie-Rose, you have an extra shopping bag around?"

CHAPTER SEVENTEEN

People must have thought I was nuts—picking up all that crap on the way to the bus. They were all used to seeing me around in that neighborhood, but I never collected junk before. I just couldn't seem to help it. When Claire mentioned flowers for Alfie, I knew then what I wanted to bring him. When I saw an old bottlecap, I picked it up and put it in the bag. Same with matchcovers, cigar rings, tin foil, anything and everything I used to see him collect. I walked with my head down, searching, and when I spotted something good, I stuck it in the bag. Not even the trash baskets were safe from me. I shared one with a lady all painted up in the face like a clown, two red circles on her cheeks and a big red smear where her lips might be. She didn't seem to have a decent, whole piece of clothing on her back. She had a couple of shopping bags filled with God knows what. I saw some newspapers sticking out of one, and from the smell, I'd say she either collected dead mice or had just eaten one.

"You lose something, sonny?" she asked me, real friendly like. One eye seemed to wander around in her head, but the other eye was anxious and fixed on me. She probably was worried that I would be after the same things she was. The last thing I wanted was a conversation, but I couldn't afford to *think* about a person like that just then—someone who looked like that and poking through trash. I couldn't spare the feeling, if you know what I mean. I was better off talking. So I said no, I was just seeing what I could find, nothing in mind.

That was something she could understand. It got her all het up. She set down her shopping bags and said, "What people throw away, you wouldn't believe. Here, look what is just from today! People are crazy to throw good stuff away!" She began to pull out things from one of her bags—one sneaker, half a cupcake in a pastry box, a little kid's broken toy, an empty tin of Lucky Strike cigarettes. I stopped her right then.

"Could I have the tin foil?" I asked. I knew the inside was lined with it.

"You collecting?" She wasn't any too ready to share.

"No. It's for a friend of mine."

She handed it over—for her, a real act of charity.

"A friend, hah? Friends you can keep. Can't trust any of them. They up and leave you holding the bag." She looked down at what she was carrying and wheezed with laughter. "Holding the bag, see?" She held it up. "Nope, can't depend on anyone but cats, I say. I have six sweeties waiting for me at home. And they'll be there when I get there. Friends leave you in the lurch, so get yourself some cats instead." She shook her head till her chins wobbled, and walked off with her bags, still shaking her head.

Poor lady, I thought. Only cats, only trash. But she was right about one thing. "Leave you in the lurch," she said, and that's the truth. Alfie. Alfie.

That was the way I got to the hospital, searching through trash baskets and picking up whatever I could find from the streets.

When I got there, I went straight to Alfie's old ward, not knowing what I would find there. His bed was empty, stripped to the mattress.

I left the bag on Alfie's bed. Let *them* dump it.

Then I went to see Mrs. Brenner. I honestly didn't know what else to do, because as I stared at Alfie's bed, Claire's question "What if?" rose in my mind. What if we hadn't taken him out this weekend? I needed first aid real bad.

Thank God she answered my knock. As soon as she opened the door, she drew me in and sat me down. She drew up a chair next to mine. "I am so very sorry, Lester," she said after our hands clung a bit. "Mr. Burt is flying in from Chicago. You want to stay here and wait for him?"

I shook my head no. I didn't want to see Alfie's father.

"Everything was done for him that could be done. The doctors just couldn't save him, you know."

I knew. It wasn't the doctors' fault. I knew whose fault it was. What a funny little person she was, so dumpy and plain looking, a pencil stuck in her hair, and stern gold-rimmed glasses that seemed to enlarge her eyes and make them even sharper. How could just being with her make me feel better? Some people have a thing about them, like an electrical charge that you could practically see, if only you had the eyesight. Lena had it, only hers was like a fourth of July sparkler while Mrs. Brenner's was steadier, deeper, no burn to it at all. Her eyes never left my face, and I could feel her with me totally.

"He couldn't help the doctors, you see. He couldn't tell them what he felt, what was wrong. He didn't have the gift of pain to help diagnose. You understand? So by the time they operated, the poisons were already through him. Nothing to be done. You must understand that, Lester."

I just nodded. That wasn't it. If he had stayed in the hospital instead of me taking him out, they might have gotten to him sooner.

Mrs. Brenner must have sensed she wasn't on the right track.

"Talk to me, Lester!"

I couldn't.

"You're blaming yourself!"

I looked at the wall and nodded.

Her finger pointed to me. "Well now, as I see it, you have a few choices here." She said this briskly, the softness all gone. "You can stew in this feeling of guilt, wear it like a hair shirt for the rest of your days. You can make it a reason, an excuse, for not doing anything with your own life, just as you were going to use Alfie himself for that. You were, you know. That's what you were doing, and if you didn't realize this before, I'm telling you now. So that's one choice. Or else you can use your head more and see that you're not to blame. No one **is.**

And go on and make Alfie's death, no, Alfie's *life*, count for something. Get on with it, for heaven's sake. Make something of yourself. Use him for that!"

This went right to an open wound. "Use! Use! That's all you're saying! I used Alfie. You don't have to tell me. I know that now. We all did, all of us. What a horrible thing. But I'm the worst. I thought it was because . . . because we were friends. I thought it was because I, I . . . ." I couldn't bear to say the word.

She said it for me. "You thought it was because of love?"

I couldn't speak, my head too heavy to lift. Mrs. Brenner rose and stood behind me to rest her hands on my shoulders. Into my ear she spoke. "So what's the difference? What's the contradiction? You can use and need and love at the same time. You think people are simple like a glass of water? We all take things from one another. What's so terrible about that? We *need* one another!"

I heard a long sigh. She left me and walked to the window. Something out there caught her eye and she beckoned to me. "Come here a minute." My legs weren't behaving, but I got there.

"See there?" She pointed to the raffle seller in the wheelchair, the one I liked to avoid, the feeble-minded C.P. So what?

"That's Charlie. Do me a favor? Go say hello to him for me. Poor devil, he's been here for years and years, put here when he was about your age. Yes, raffles and newspapers for him," she said, nodding, held by the sight.

136

Then once again she was all business. "Look, Lester, I've got a million things to do before Mr. Burt arrives. If you don't want to see him, why don't you go home now. And do yourself a favor! Go on back to school!"

"Why?"

"Because that's where the learning is. You want to sell raffles all your life?"

She saw me to the door. "Come back to see me." She stood on tiptoes and kissed my cheek.

Outside in the sunshine, I stood on the steps and took a deep breath of air. It was filled with the smell of turned-over earth between the cement paths.

What I felt like doing was to slump on the sun-warmed steps and take a long nap. My head felt so stuffed with things to think about it was like having a head cold. I looked across the way at the other building where Alfie once lived. The scene of the big kidnapping. It must have taken place in some other life, it seemed so long ago.

On the steps, I thought I saw .... But it couldn't be, because I left her back in the kitchen with Claire! Tillie-Rose! She wasn't due at the hospital till later.

I couldn't yell. Tried to wave and couldn't do that, either. Even so, she saw me and yelled, "Lester!" All heads turned as if on signal her way. She waved wildly and started over to me.

I was so immensely glad to see her. I *needed* her. I needed her big heart. I was going to *use* her, use her comfort and friendship to help make me feel better. She was dear to me!

"Claire and Alex went off, and I couldn't bear to have

137

you here alone. You mad at me?" Tillie-Rose looked a
mess, but to me, she was the very image of an oasis, of
water to a very thirsty person.

"You go up to see Alfie?" she asked, not knowing how
else to account for how dazed I must have looked.

"He's not there, Tillie-Rose. He's not any place. His
father is coming to make arrangements, I guess. I suppose there'll be a funeral and all. Hey, can you skip your
volunteer work today and go home with me? We'll go
to the beach?"

"Sure. You bet. Anything, Les."

"Wait a minute. See that guy over there, the one in
the wheelchair selling raffles? I told Mrs. Brenner I'd
say hello."

We walked across the path, back to Alfie's building
where Charlie tried to sell something to all the visitors
coming in and out.

He had a tray in front of him like a baby's high chair,
piled with papers and booklets.

"Hi, Charlie," I said.

"How . . . do . . . you . . . know . . . my . . . name?"
Big spaces between his words to make room for the con-
tortions of his face to get the next one out. It was pain-
ful for me to see. I wasn't as bad as that, but it was
close enough.

"Mrs. Brenner told me."

"You . . . are . . . Alfie's . . . friend. I . . . am . . . sorry."

I was ready to go. I had had enough. But then Charlie
began to talk about Alfie. Other people in wheelchairs
drew near and chimed in. One of their number had died,
and it was like a service for him. What they wanted was

to tell one another and to tell me that Alfie was a good boy, a good person, that he would be missed. Always ready to push a chair or go to the canteen for them. "Not a mean bone in his body," said the half-person I once called Miss Pink Bow.

"He's better out of it," said an old man sunk in his chair, muffled to his ears, his head unable to stop its shaking.

"Well out of it," I heard all around me. "Yes, yes, better off." They were all in agreement.

"No . . . he . . . is . . . not," said Charlie. Then, in his drawn and twisted way, he told us how he had planned to share his business with Alfie, make him his partner. "He . . . was . . . special."

He could see that? I hung on to Charlie's every word, absolutely astounded. I thought he was a dummy, retarded, way, way different from me. And then, listening to him, I could see that the only real difference between Charlie and me was that I was able to leave and he wasn't. That I had choices and he didn't. Only the wheelchair separated us. Only my determination to never, not ever, be in that wheelchair.

"Come on, let's go," I said to Tillie-Rose, pulling on her arm.

"You . . . are . . . on . . . your . . . way?" Charlie asked me.

"Yes, I am."

DATE DUE

FEB 13 1984			

83-67